The Lightness of Air

ANGELA MILLER-ROTHBART

texture.
PUBLISHING

The Lightness of Air

First published by Texture Publishing (Pty) Ltd

Second edition published by Newly Media (Pty) Ltd

Third edition published by Texture Publishing (Pty) Ltd

Copyright © 2022 Angela Miller-Rothbart

First edition 2022, Second edition 2022, Third edition 2023

ISBN 978-0-7961-0460-1
ISBN 978-0-7961-0461-8 (e-book)

Editors: Fiona Rom and Lorem Ipsum (Pty) Ltd
Cover design and typesetting: Texture Publishing (Pty) Ltd
Set in Warnock Pro 11/17

For Henia Bryer

"A worthy woman who can find? For her price is far above rubies." Proverbs 31:10

This is a novel. Only the historical characters and events are real, all other characters are fictitious. However, this work has been inspired by real stories of Holocaust survivors whom I have known.

You may shoot me with your words,
You may cut me with your eyes,
You may kill me with your hatefulness,
But still, like air, I'll rise.

from
Still I Rise
– Maya Angelou

Authors Note

Dear Reader

"The past is never dead. It is not even past."

These words of William Faulkner echoed in my memory the day I met Henia Bryer.

I met Henia through the Jewish Seniors club. Recently retired from a large business that initially began out of my baby's pram due to the lack of a car, I found myself with too much time on my hands. So I signed up as a volunteer with the Jewish seniors. Soon afterwards I was contacted by the director, inviting me to meet Henia. Since that phone call so many years ago, I have often pondered how something as innocuous as a phone call could have had such a profound effect.

Now a nonagenarian, Henia grew up in Poland and is a survivor of the Holocaust that took place during World War II. She survived being interned in several concentration camps: Majdanek, Auschwitz and Breslau. Henia also survived the horror of a march in freezing temperatures, which took three days and three nights to the infamous Bergen-Belsen camp, considered the harshest of all the concentration camps. The march became known as the Death March. After being liberated in mid 1945, Henia managed to reach Palestine with 'legal documents' obtained through the underground and fought in the 1948 War of Independence which led to the establishment of the state of Israel.

This is Henia's story – a chronicle of strength, courage and resilience. As our friendship has grown over many meetings during the past decade, I have come to realise that it is not just the Holocaust that defines this gracious woman. There are so many other facets to her and I have been privileged, through her evocative story telling, to live the past through her and with her.

"No matter how many books you read or how many movies you see, you will never know what it was like unless you were there."

These are Henia's words and therefore I accept the fact that there is a wounded place deep within her that I will never reach.

While age has bestowed Henia with its own beauty, there is something about her aura of dignity and serenity that first drew me to her.

It took a while before she opened up to me and related the stories of her youth and of the war years but when she did, it was as if I was being swept back to the past. I was not just hearing these stories but watching them unfold before me.

POLAND 1938:

Henia is a bright young student at the Gymnasium, or college as it is better known. She and her family, her mother, father, two brothers and a sister live in a comfortable apartment where a cook prepares lavish meals. 'Tata' owns a leather shoe factory and the children's shoes and clothing are bespoke items. During the winter months, they enjoyed ice skating on the frozen lakes, in summer, holidaying in a villa by the riverside are among the many pleasures of her childhood.

Yet all this is about to change.

1939: GERMANY INVADES POLAND

In my imagination, I stand with her and her family outside their home under the watchful eyes of the Nazi soldiers. Each family member carries a small parcel. These are the only belongings that they are allowed to take with them to the Radom Ghetto. In my mind's eye, we watch the Nazis loot their home and carry away their possessions, including Henia's precious piano. Her tears elicit no sympathy from the soldiers.

My heart clenches because I know that soon half of this family will be murdered.

I try to imagine standing for hours in the back of a cattle truck in freezing, sub-zero temperatures with the remaining survivors of the death march but ... this much I cannot do.

I wonder aloud: How did any of those interned in the concentration camps manage to survive the unspeakable cruelty inflicted on such innocent people? I ask these questions and my answers come across as a shadow passing over Henia's face, a tightening of her throat or a flicker in her eyes. This tells me more than words can.

I ask: *What happened to your little sister?*

She says: *She walked into the gas chamber.*

I ask: *How do you know?*

She says: *I watched her go.*

The words of Zelda Fitzpatrick came back to me:

"No one has ever measured, not even poets, how much the human heart can hold."

A few years after the War of Independence, Henia arrived in Bloemfontein, South Africa as a young bride, having married Maurice Bryer in Israel. She taught herself to speak English and embarked on a teaching career. Over time she rose through the ranks to become the head mistress of the Jewish School in the Orange Free State. All this while raising two fine sons of whom she is justifiably very proud.

I am captivated by these stories of her younger self but I am not surprised. Henia has a daunting intellect and her retelling of history has kept me spellbound.

Still there is one story that touches me deeply.

Henia is part of a group of young girls newly arrived in Auschwitz. It is Yom Kippur. The Nazis 'aktions' were meted out on auspicious Jewish festivals. The girls were faced with a pile of shoes as high as a small mountain. The incensed Nazi officer, brandishing a baton, insisted that the girls separate the shoes into pairs. As this was an impossible task, the girls held hands and formed a circle and sang "*Das ist der schonste tag meines lebens*" (This is the most beautiful day of my life). It had the effect of calming the irate soldier.

I am often asked why the "*Lightness of Air*" is a novel and not written as Henia's memoir.

Having signed up with the Jewish Seniors, I simultaneously joined a writing group. Henia's stories had such a powerful impact on me that I recorded them, sharing them with the members of the group. They urged me to publish these stories. However, Henia had not asked me to write her memoir and I was acutely aware of not invading her privacy or breaking her trust in our friendship. Thus I created fictitious characters in a novel inspired by her life, in which I interspersed some of the real stories of the concentration camps as related to me by Henia.

As my novel was progressing I felt it was time to read it to her. She listened intently and then she turned to me and said *"publish it and dedicate it to me"*.

It was that pivotal moment that breathed life into *"The Lightness of Air"*.

Since the end of World War II, the words *"Lest we forget"* and *"Never again"* have become a mantra. Unless the stories of Henia Bryer and other survivors are passed down to future generations, there is the danger that the world will forget and that "never again" will be just a fleeting dream.

"There is no path. The path is made by walking," said the Spanish poet Antonio Machado.

Henia Bryer, my inspiration, is a fitting example.

With love,
ANGELA MILLER-ROTHBART

Prologue

It has been there all day. The long white envelope is weathered with age, the familiar script on the front faded but still legible. That, and the foreign stamp, indicate to her what it is certain to contain.

Helena is sitting at her desk. The slanting rays of the afternoon sun gild the room and pool on the envelope, giving it a translucent appearance. It beckons to her, daring her to break the seal. She is aware that the contents could alter her life, and she knows how swiftly the world can tumble and change.

Succumbing to its seductiveness, Helena reaches for the envelope. She runs her fingertips across the smooth texture of the paper, then at arm's length, she holds it up to the light.

This is my connection between past and present, but will it only deepen old wounds?

Fear slows down her breathing.

And then she breaks the seal, and the contents tumble out onto the desk. Images of a distant past and fragments of Polish text dance before her eyes, evoking memories so powerful that she feels as though time is suspended.

She tucks a loose tendril of silvering hair behind her ear and adjusts her spectacles. With a sigh of resignation, she straightens her shoulders.

It is time to face the past.

PART ONE

Chapter 1

POLAND

SEPTEMBER 1939

The day began as any other. Shafts of golden sunlight seeped through the windowpanes of the house on Polna Street, flooding it with light and draining away the shadows of the night. The bustling sounds coming from the kitchen and the smell of freshly baked bread heralded the start of a new day in the Jablonski household.

But with the break of day, the skies darkened with German planes that looped and dipped over the rooftops as they screeched through the air.

In the small Polish town, men and women clustered in groups on street corners. The news was electrifying. Germany had invaded Poland. Their hope that this would not happen slowly crumbled when they saw fear reflected in each other's eyes. A sense of foreboding settled over the usually peaceful town as residents scuttled to the security of their homes, not knowing what to expect.

The sounds of impending war had been rattling, spectrelike, around the town for a while but there'd been an obstinate belief that this would not happen. "It won't happen", they had said. "We have been through wars before", they'd said. Now the ominous sound of marching boots, the rumbling of trucks through the town and orders being bellowed over loudhailers confirmed their worst fears and shattered their hopes. Within hours the new laws became a reality.

For the first time the children did not go to school.

Close by, they skipped rope. Their parents' hushed voices had sheltered them from the reality of war and they felt secure in the unchanged rhythms of their lives and the fulfilment of their dreams. Among the group, Helena Jablonski skipped with her friend Sofia, their pigtails flying behind them, until the voices of anxious mothers called to their children to come indoors.

Their world was beginning to shrink as their hopes diminished. But in the Jablonski home preparations for the high festival of Rosh Hashana, just weeks away, were still being carried out.

Pots had been bubbling on the kitchen stove for days. Cook Berta, her sleeves rolled up to her elbows, was armed with a wooden spoon with which she vigorously stirred the contents of the pots, her other hand firmly placed on her ample hip. She was preparing the traditional festival dishes of roast turkey, brisket cooked with carrots and prunes, herrings and sumptuous honey cakes baked in the baker's oven. The smells of her cooking wafted temptingly throughout the apartment.

For the two days of the festival, all the family members, including a myriad of uncles, aunts and cousins, would gather in the apartment for the evening meal after synagogue. There would be lively conversation, much laughter and robust singing late into the night, until the littlest children fell asleep and would have to be carried home.

There was much to prepare.

The long rosewood dining room table had been polished until it gleamed. The white linen tablecloths had been starched and ironed with the heavy copper iron that Nanny Olga heated on the coal stove. Fragrance from the lavender-scented water used to dampen the cloths before ironing, floated through the air. The Oleander trees in their ornamental pots that stood at either end of the spacious hallway had been cut and trimmed. All was ready to greet the guests.

Beneath the apartment, a cellar housed the preserves and pickles that had been prepared throughout the year, for the festival, and also as provisions for the freezing, snowbound winter months. How Helena looked forward to the moment when Cook would take her hand and lead her down to the cool, dimly-lit cellar. Shiny jars of apples, plums, pears and cherries and a variety of vegetables lined the shelves. Cook would open a jar of cherries and select the biggest one for Helena and she would bite into the sweet, succulent fruit, the ripe cherry juice trickling down her chin.

The English lessons with her tutor, Hilda, to which she submitted reluctantly, had been suspended until after the festival. Mameh and Tateh dismissed her protests about having to spend time after school hours mastering the English language; she would rather have been skating with the other children on the frozen ponds than taking instruction from a stern Hilda. But Tateh was wise.

"The day will come when you will thank me for these lessons, Helena," he said sternly, holding up both his hands to indicate the end of the discussion.

He could never have foreseen the outcome of his prediction nor how many times Helena would hear the echo of these words. But for that moment, with lessons suspended, she delighted in the extra time she could spend with Cook, rearranging the jars on the shelves.

Mameh had been to Vienna and had brought back new clothes for Helena and her younger sister Eva to wear for the festival. Helena never tired of stroking the soft, silky dresses, skirts and tunics in a rainbow of colours. She caressed the ermine fur trim on the woollen coat and matching muff, and tingled with the anticipation of wearing these garments.

The wait for the festival seemed endless to Helena.

Tateh is the owner of a shoe factory and before every festival he takes her to the factory to select a pair of shoes to complete her new outfits from Vienna. Yesterday was that day, the day she had most looked forward to.

There was a time when he called her 'my little girl' but now Tateh calls her 'my young lady'. Now that she is a young lady she walks sedately by Tateh's side, holding his hand, all the way to the factory. Where his name – Rudi Jablonski – is painted in bold red letters above the entrance. The smell of leather hangs heavy in the air from the moment they enter through the wooden doorway. It is the same smell that lingers on Tateh when he returns home from the factory each evening. She calls it her Tateh-smell, and she revels in the feeling of security that it brings to her.

Mr Dudek, the factory manager, greeted her warmly with his arms held wide open. He pats the top of her head and, widening his eyes, he exclaims: "Look how much you have grown." Now that she is almost grown up, he shakes her hand solemnly, enclosing her little hand in his large, rough one.

Helena was dazzled by the rows of leather shoes. Mr Dudek led her past shelves laden with shoes for young ladies, in many colours and designs. She frowned in concentration, trying to decide which she most liked, until she spotted a pair of shiny black patent leather pumps with just the hint of a heel. She stopped in front of the shelf and nodded her head at Mr Dudek while pointing at the pair that she had selected. He slipped the shoes onto her feet and made notes of the necessary adjustments in the large notebook that he carried with him.

Mr Dudek and Helena shared a secret. Although Helena was not yet fully grown, her feet were and her large feet were a constant source of embarrassment. Peering over his shoulder, Helena smiled with satisfaction when she observed him make a note in his book to mark her shoes two sizes smaller than they were. Then he winked at her and she knew that her secret with Mr Dudek was safe. He assured Helena that the shoes would be ready in time for her to wear for the festival.

Before they left the factory, Tateh reminded her of the days when she was still his little girl, his 'Mameleh' – little darling – when he would swing her up on to his shoulders and dance her around the factory floor. She would laugh so hard that she would have to tighten her hold on Tateh's neck so as not to fall off his shoulders, but he always kept her safe. Once she had chosen a pair of shoes, they would leave the factory and he would continue to carry her on his shoulders all the way back to the apartment, both of them singing with gusto.

The memory makes her nestle against Tateh's side in contentment, knowing that she will always be his little girl no matter how tall she grows.

When they arrived back at the apartment and entered the front door, Mameh reminded them to cover their shoes with the felt overshoes that were kept beneath the coat rack. The wooden oak floors of the apartment had been polished until they shone like mirrors and Mameh feared that Tateh's muddy boots would leave marks on the shiny surfaces. Although Mameh barely reached Tateh's shoulder, he would never defy her orders. He loved her and would often tell her so.

Eva was waiting with Mameh to greet Tateh and Helena. Tomorrow it would be her chance to visit the factory with Tateh to select a pair of shoes and, after all, she was still his little girl.

This evening, Maestro Trotsky will come to their home. His nimble fingers will run across the keys of the majestic grand piano that stands in the vast reception area and then, with Helena's wrists poised above the keys, he will encourage her to play the same melodies.

In the coming weeks, the Jablonski family would watch in

horror and helplessness as Nazi officers carry this piano as well as their other possessions out of their home.

But now Mameh and Tateh sway in unison to the music, awed by their beautiful and gifted daughter. After music lessons, Cook Berta serves dinner – Helena's favourite borscht and dumplings and herbed roasts, and then the best part of the meal, Berta's own invention of sweet desserts. Eva struggles to hold the heavy silver cutlery under the watchful eye of Tateh.

Later, Helena slips beneath the cover of the goose down comforter specially stitched for her by Abram the tailor. The girls sleep soundly in the room they share, dreaming of their summer holiday at the family's riverside villa. Life has always ticked by as reliably as the giant grandfather clock that stands sentinel in the hallway, predicting a safe and secure future for this family.

Only, that is not to be.

At the end of the day, as the sun slips over the horizon and nightfall bruises the sky, the unwelcome guest, the spectre of war, infiltrates the home of the Jablonski family.

Their lives are forever changed.

Chapter 2

BERGEN-BELSEN, GERMANY
MAY 1945

She drifted in and out of consciousness, only dimly aware of the tangle of bodies and the low moans of the sick and dying that surrounded her. Visions of her family still alive floated before her, their arms outstretched, imploring her to stay in their warm embrace. But then, mercifully, the darkness drew her in, obliterating the stark reality of her shattered world.

The camp had been liberated but typhus was rampant. Medical officers and soldiers, fearful of becoming infected, abandoned the inmates until the assistance of more experienced doctors eventually arrived. The Nazis had fled, leaving more destruction in their wake: attempting to destroy all signs of their barbarism, they had blown up the crematoria. Even the most hardened of soldiers who entered the camp were unprepared for the scale of human tragedy that awaited them. Some of the soldiers vomited while others fainted at the stench of charred remains.

Through the fog of consciousness, she hears voices that grow louder as they come closer. A hand gently prods at her. Reluctantly she opens heavy-lidded eyes and peers into the blurred features of a young soldier. Eyes filled with pity look back at her. The soldier leans in so close, she can feel his breath on her skin.

"What is your name?" he asks.

Through parched and cracked lips she whispers, "Helena Jablonski."

Painfully she raises her stick-thin arms, the numbered tattoo clearly visible on the inside of her left wrist, and with her hands she cups the soldier's face. She feels his warm tears seep between her icy fingers.

"This one's alive," he calls, his voice thick with emotion. Like a puppet whose strings have been cut, she is lifted up by a pair of sturdy arms. Slowly turning her head, she is struck by the sight of the heavy iron gates that imprisoned her and her fellow inmates in Bergen-Belsen now flung wide open. Spidery threads of sunlight filter through the gloomy air, air which is dense with the smell of death and destruction.

And then Helena knows, that despite all the horror she has endured, she has survived.

Days blurred into weeks as Helena fought the illness that wracked her body, clinging to a thin cord of life. Barely-human forms moved around the camp like ghosts. Hollow-eyed and emaciated, their bones were visible through their pale, transparent skin. The sadistic guards had been replaced by kinder soldiers and medics, but they were inexperienced and their kindness could spell death for those survivors who were unable to tolerate the rich food they were fed. The qualified doctors who eventually arrived knew how to treat the disease-ravished inmates, and attempted to offer them comfort and solace. But for damaged souls with broken lives and uncertain futures, there was neither comfort nor solace.

As Helena struggled through the smog of illness, memories surfaced unbidden, wrapping themselves around her. The longing for her family and the security of her world on Polna Street drew her into an abyss of melancholy.

And yet her desire to live was charged by the belief that she was destined to chronicle to the world the atrocities that had been inflicted on an innocent and helpless people.

She would live to tell the world. A world that stood silently by, watching – complicit.

Chapter 3

BERGEN-BELSEN, GERMANY

SUMMER 1945

The icy chill of war that had gripped the world was beginning to loosen its hold. The long-awaited summer generously showered its warmth on a world that had grown frigid with suffering. This warmth seeped into Helena's limbs, fuelling her recovery and reaffirming her resolve to embrace the unknown as an orphan. When she was a spirited young girl, she nurtured visions of a fulfilled destiny as a concert pianist, and now, as the iciness in her heart began to thaw, she clung to these dreams.

The days drifted by bringing a feeling of renewed energy. The indisputable fact that the war was finally over created a sense of awareness among the survivors of the possibility of hope. The contorted reality of their existence was replaced with a yearning to pick up the pieces of their broken lives in a broken world.

In the aftermath of war and the chaos that ensued, a new chapter was unfolding. A myriad of disseminated souls, lost and helpless, had been released from camps all over Poland and Germany. Desperately they searched for surviving family members, hoping to be reunited. Mostly their searches were in vain, but when contact was made it brought heart-wrenching reunions.

It was evening in the camp, the air still warm. With the aid of the doctors Helena was recovering and slowly regaining her strength. Basking in the warm summer air, she was encouraged to take her first tentative steps. It was then that she heard her name being called. She felt her pulse quicken as the familiar voice exploded in her memory.

Turning, she froze in disbelief at the figure before her, for there stood Sofia, her childhood friend with whom she had skipped rope on Polna Street so long ago. Mutely the two women stared at each other.

Through a knot of tears Helena whispered, "Sofia, can it be you?"

Hesitantly she reached out to touch her friend's face and then they fell into each other's arms, their tears mingling. Questions collided as the two friends held onto each other, reunited.

"Sofia, can it be true that you are alive and here with me?" Helena repeated. She was stunned at the physical appearance of her friend. Once fresh-faced and plump-cheeked, Sofia was dramatically changed. Bald and bone-thin, her features were haggard and her skin sallow. Helena ran her hand over the prickly stubbles of regrowth on her own scalp and shivered with the realisation that Sofia mirrored her own image.

"How did you find me, Sofia?" she asked.

"The lists," Sofia replied. "The names of survivors of our town are kept at the American Zone." She describes a chaotic scene of people aimlessly wandering around seeking names, all of them needing help, pushing and pulling at each other to read the lists placed up on boards. Somehow, in this melee, she'd found Helena's name.

"Eventually I managed to get a ride with a Russian soldier back to the camp, hoping you would still be here. Now that I have found you, we must leave."

"Dearest Helena, we are free."

Chapter 4

BERGEN-BELSEN - BRITISH ZONE, GERMANY
SUMMER 1945

Bergen-Belsen had been liberated by the British, so this area of Northern Germany had become known as the British Zone. Similarly, the American and French liberators established Zones across Germany. Displaced persons without any documentation or possessions made their way to one of the Zones to receive clothing, accommodation and other basic requirements.

Helena and Sofia remained at the British Zone long enough to regain their strength. They consoled each other as they shared stories of unimaginable suffering.

"Sofia, your family lived close to mine on Polna Street. What happened to them?" Helena asked, gently taking Sofia's hand in her own.

Thoughts so painful clouded Sofia's eyes and her words came out heavy.

"We were having our evening meal when we heard boots marching up to our front door. My father unpinned the chain of his gold watch and handed it to my mother before the soldiers burst in. 'Borzina,' he said. 'You will need this. I have no more use for it.' And then he was pushed out the door at gunpoint. We heard a single shot ring out in the quiet night.

"Then they came for us – my mother, my sister Anna, and me. We were sent on cattle trucks to Majdanek where we were separated. I didn't see my mother again, but I did see Anna. She was among a group of children led by a rabbi, being marched into a gas chamber. As they entered the chamber, I heard the rabbi intone the prayer, 'Hear O Israel, the Lord is God, the Lord is One'."

Helena wrapped her arms around Sofia, the ache in her heart erupting in her chest.

"Now we have only each other. But what happened to your family?" Sophia asked, her throat constricted with tears. Helena drew a long, deep breath to quiet the racing pulse of her heart. Sofia's question, so burdensome, drew her back to her life in the ghetto and she remained contemplative before answering.

"My father was shot while trying to escape through the ghetto wall at night. He hoped to barter the few coins we had managed to hide, for food. Eva and I were sent as slave labourers to work in a factory, mending the German soldiers' uniforms. One morning, Eva, handling a very heavy hot iron, scorched an officer's shirt. She was shot in front of me. Days later my mother and I were sent to Auschwitz, where we were separated. I continued to search for my mother, but I never saw her again."

And so, the two solitary souls, bonded in their suffering, their friendship strengthened by their painful pasts, planned a path forward for their shared futures.

Chapter 5

GERMANY

After careful deliberation, Helena and Sofia decided to make the American Zone their destination. They hoped that the Americans could provide them with the names of relatives and friends, as many survivors from their town had gathered there.

So it happened, on a sultry summer morning, under a sky bleached with sunlight, that Helena at last turned her back on the hell that had been Bergen-Belsen. The finality of walking freely through the gates lit a dark corner of her soul. With time that light would grow to illuminate the life of the woman she was yet to become. But in that moment, the emotional damage inflicted upon her during her long internment lay dormant. Like a creeping tide, it would gather strength and flow into every crevice of her being, leaving behind the detritus of haunted memories and tortured dreams.

All of this was yet to manifest. In this spectacular moment she was free, the road before her wide open and the future beckoned enticingly.

Barefoot, gaunt, their striped prison uniforms exchanged for fresh, if ill-fitting, clothing, the friends began a journey that in the fullness of time would take Helena to the far-flung corners of the globe.

It was the dawn of their new reality.

Friendly Allied soldiers were plentiful along the way, eager to greet them and offer advice. Soon a dusty green army truck drew up alongside them.

"Hop in, gals. Where y'all heading?" drawled the young GI good-naturedly.

"To the American Zone."

"You're in luck, ladies. Heading that way myself, but you'll have to hoof it for the last bit. Got some extra grub too."

Unhesitatingly they clambered into the vehicle, as grateful for the black bread and bologna as they were for the comfort of the ride. The young soldier was eager to answer their questions and to fill in the gaps about aspects of the war unknown to them. In stunned silence, the women absorbed the magnitude of Pearl Harbour and the part played by Eisenhower and Churchill in ending the hostilities. Japan had staged a surprise attack, forcing America to join the war.

Helena remembered the long hours she had reluctantly spent with her English tutor. How useful those lessons had now become. Remembering her father's words, she silently thanked Tateh and Mameh for insisting that she learned to speak English.

"This is it, gals," said the soldier as he brought the truck to a screeching halt. "This is as far as I go. A fifteen-minute walk will get you to the American Zone."

The women climbed down, and with a toothy grin the soldier doffed his cap flamboyantly and sped off in a cloud of dust.

The sun was at its zenith, beating down relentlessly as Helena and Sofia continued on their way. Berlin was littered with the carnage and devastation of war. Most of Europe had been demolished. Victims of Nazi atrocities milled around, their aim was to make their way to America or Palestine. Returning to their shattered homes was not an option; most of the towns had vanished. Once beautiful and vibrant villages were reduced to charred remains and the townsfolk murdered. The survivors were not welcome in almost all countries. Many longed to leave the blood-soaked soil of Europe with its stench of death for Palestine, but the British embargo prohibited this.

Helena and Sofia linked arms as they set off on the last part of their journey. Signposts marked their way. As they reached the boundary of the American Zone, Sofia gave a sharp cry of pain and stumbled against Helena.

"Sofia, are you ill?" Helena's voice rang out in alarm. All the colour has drained from Sofia's face and her features were twisted in pain.

"My feet," gasped Sofia.

It was only then, when she looked closely, that Helena became aware of the blackened skin of Sofia's toes, the discolouration creeping up her feet.

Tenderly Helena cradled her friend, who was weightless as a child. "What has happened to your feet?" Helena cried.

Through gasps of pain, Sofia's story unfolded. During her internment, she carefully guarded her one pair of shoes. At night she slept with them beneath her head, but the shoes were stolen by another inmate during the night. When the Russians were on the brink of liberating the camps, she was forced to walk barefoot in the snow for days towards Bergen-Belsen, along with other prisoners, in what became known as the Death March.

The young medics attending to the remnants of the inmates that had reached Bergen-Belsen wanted to operate on Sofia's damaged feet, but a friend who had previously been a nurse came to her aid. She believed that if the inexperienced medics were to operate, they would leave Sofia crippled, so she hid her young friend away from the medics and treated her frost-bitten feet. Using an old Polish remedy, she immersed Sofia's blackened feet repeatedly in alternate buckets of ice-cold and boiling-hot water and then applied a thick black paste. This painful procedure brought Sofia a measure of relief but the damage to her frostbitten feet was irreversible and slowly the ache had returned.

Until that moment, she had been able to contain the agony of frostbite. But her reservoir of resilience was spent and she finally surrendered to the pain that engulfed her, slipping into unconsciousness.

Helena sank to the ground cradling Sofia's head in her lap, frantically calling out for help. It didn't take long for her cries to be answered.

Medical interns working in a nearby makeshift hospital tent heard her cries and rushed to their aid. Strong and capable arms carried Sofia into the cool sanctuary of the mud-coloured hospital tent and into the care of Doctor Luca Rossi. The middle-aged doctor had thinning hair and wore a crisp white jacket. He had a commanding presence but his deep-blue eyes were pools of compassion. The kindly doctor immediately took charge of Sofia and settled Helena into a comfortable armchair. After the years of cruelty that Helena had endured, the care shown to her felt like the sun breaking through storm clouds. Gratefully she sipped the tepid tea she was given. The emotions of the day's events swirled around her until her eyelids grew heavy, too heavy to lift. A sense of peace washed over her and she slipped into sleep.

Threads of moonlight trailed across the night sky when Helena awoke. Her eyes fluttered open, absorbing her surroundings. Dr Luca was sprawled in a chair across from her, his long legs stretched before him, his white jacket crumpled from having been slept in. He gazed thoughtfully at Helena, wearily rubbing his thumb and forefinger across his eyes.

"Your friend is gravely ill," he said, his tone measured. "Typhus has affected her lungs. I will do my best to save her feet, but it is going to be a long journey with no assured outcome. Too many lives have been lost on the altar of German greed; my team will fight to prevent the loss of another one."

A flood of emotions engulfed Helena as she abandoned the last vestiges of sleep and reality curled itself around her. Sofia had become her beacon of courage and support, and the thought of leaving her behind in the care of the doctor filled Helena with despair. Clearly, she would have to continue her journey alone.

It would be many months before it would be known whether Sophia would ever walk again.

Chapter 6

THE AMERICAN ZONE
SUMMER 1945

Dawn cast an amber glow over the hospital tent as Helena awoke, having dozed off during the night in a chair next to Sofia's bed. The interns were preparing breakfast and the fragrant smell of coffee filled the tent. She stretched her cramped limbs and rubbed the sleep from her eyes, trying to remember where she was. Dr Luca urged the girls to tuck into the meal that the interns had prepared. Sofia ate sparingly, every mouthful encouraged by the doctor. Helena ate with relish, devouring the wedges of cheese, thick slices of buttered bread and scrambled eggs, surprised at how hungry she was.

As the time came for her to leave, she held onto Sofia, stroking her cheek.

"I will never abandon you, Sofia. I will be back soon," she murmured.

"It is best that you go now, Lenie." Sofia's eyes shone with unshed tears as she called Helena by her childhood name. "I will follow you as soon as I am well."

With one last embrace, Helena prepared to leave. Waving farewell to Dr Luca and his team of interns, she set out, her bare feet leaving imprints in the dusty road.

Sofia watched Helena's retreating figure through a gap in the hospital tent until it dwindled and became too small to be seen.

Alone Helena reached the offices of the American Zone where she was welcomed by the officials of yet another displaced persons' camp. She was soon absorbed into its throbbing rhythm. A myriad of stateless people roamed the area, wounded souls waiting to be claimed. A feeling of despair permeated the air.

The American organisation Joint, also known as JDC or the Joint Distribution Committee, was founded in 1914 to provide humanitarian assistance to Jews worldwide. It was active in the area. Volunteers worked constantly, assisting survivors to connect with family members and generously supplying accommodation, food, and clothing. Such kindness reaffirmed Helena's belief that it was worth the gruelling journey that she and Sophia had undertaken.

She was accommodated in a cottage which she shared with Rachel, a German Jewish woman. Rachel had survived the war hidden in the basement of the home of her German neighbour, Hans Grun. She was the only surviving member of her family, all of whom perished in the Nazi death camps. Rachel was a matronly figure and had retained her dignity despite all she had endured. She radiated an inner strength that drew Helena to her, and a bond was formed between the two women that was cemented by loss and loneliness. It was a bond that would endure through all the vicissitudes of their lives.

Determined to return the generosity of her hosts in the camp, Helena offered her assistance to the officials in the administration office. Her ability to translate German files into English for the American soldiers and volunteers kept her in demand. She became a favourite among them, and often remained behind at the end of the day, working until late into the evenings.

Rachel, though short in stature, was an accomplished cook and her skills were put to use in the kitchen where she was regularly seen bustling around efficiently.

Max Harris was a young American volunteer enlisted with Joint. He was from New York where he had completed his second year of a law degree at Cornell University, distinguishing himself academically as well as on the sports field. His ready smile revealed deep dimples, while his athletic build and boyish good looks had increased his acceptance within Cornell's social circle.

His Russian immigrant parents, Samuel and Yetta Harris, were immensely proud of their American-born son Max, and his younger sister Gloria. Samuel had achieved financial success since arriving on the shores of America. It was only through their children that Samuel and Yetta felt that they had finally been integrated into American society.

The devastating accounts of the evil unleashed on Jews that flowed out of Europe at the end of the war deeply disturbed Max. When Joint called for volunteers to go to Berlin to assist with rehabilitation of survivors of the death camps, Max impulsively put his law degree on hold and with his parents' blessing, enlisted.

In Berlin he was welcomed by the agents of Joint and sent to the offices of the American Zone. His academic abilities were noted and he was given administrative duties in the office, analysing files that had been left behind by the Germans. The Nazis had destroyed most of the files when it became clear that they were losing the war, as though destroying information could destroy the truth. However, the Allies had uncovered files stashed away in private homes, some stitched into furniture, which provided precious information about Jews, many of them children, who had been murdered. It filled Max with horror to read these accounts, especially those concerning children and babies, that were meticulously tabulated by the Nazis.

It was the end of another gruelling day in the office and Max was still hunched over the files on his desk. The daily cacophony of sound caused by the clattering of typewriters and the ringing of telephones was silenced. He uncurled his back and rubbed his aching neck. It was then he noticed that although all the soldiers and volunteers who worked with him in the office had left, the lone figure of a girl remained at the far end of the room. She was bent over her desk, pen in hand, her tongue running across her upper lip as she concentrated on the files before her.

He strode across to her desk. "Why are you still here when everyone has already left?" he asked.

"This is the last file of the day." She sighed. "I am translating it into English. It is important because it is one that was documented by Himmler, the commander of the SS." She put down her pen and looked up at him.

In that moment, the stars charted their course. He gazed at the fragility in the depths of her eyes. The pallor of her cheeks and her close-cropped hair left him in no doubt that she was a survivor of the death camps. It stirred up emotions that had been dormant within him. At the intensity of his gaze, the girl flushed, lowering her eyes.

"What is your name?" he asked.

"Helena Jablonski," she replied softly, her eyes still downcast.

"I am Max Harris," he said, extending his hand. Recognising the tattoo on the inside of her forearm confirmed his belief that she was a survivor.

"I will wait for you until you have finished that file, and then I'll walk home with you," said Max, enquiring where she stayed before settling himself into a nearby chair. Happily, he noted that the hostel in which he was accommodated was close to the cottage that Helena shared with Rachel.

In the days that followed, Max worked closely with Helena in the office, documenting the German files. He was astonished at the quick mind of this wraithlike girl as she translated the files from German into English and added up lists of figures for the Joint officers.

He waited for Helena each evening after the day's work was completed. Together they walked to the cottage where Rachel would welcome them. Despite their long working hours, they gathered around the wooden kitchen table and shared the day's events. Rachel would prepare a pot of thick borscht and potato latkes, crisp and sizzling from the pan, for their supper. As the days went by she watched over Helena with a motherly satisfaction as Helena's gaunt frame gradually filled out. They both looked forward to Max's company and as their friendship developed, it felt as though they were bonding as a family.

Helena's small, sparsely furnished bedroom in the cottage would become her sanctuary and at the end of each exhausting day she embraced its tranquillity. It was only in the still of the night and in the fragments of her dreams that she was transported back to the horror of the life she had experienced in the camps. She was haunted by the memory of the freezing January mornings.

Helena, together with the other women, was forced to plait reed baskets that would hold German bombs. Their hands froze in the icy water in which the reeds were stored to keep them supple. Working outside in the frigid air, their fingers were soon frostbitten, but the quotas of baskets for the day had to be completed. The younger women helped the older ones to complete their quotas, so that they wouldn't be severely punished or even shot.

The memory of that fear rose up inside her in her dreams, causing her to cry out in her sleep. Hearing her cries, Rachel would sit beside her and smooth the damp hair off her clammy forehead.

"Hush, little one," she would croon soothingly until Helena's night tremors receded and slumber returned.

The ebb and flow of life continued as the days merged together.

Helena was preparing for bed when Rachel called to her. She patted the bed, indicating to Helena to sit beside her.

"*Schatzi*, it is time for me to share with you the events that have brought me here. You have had so much to bear that I did not want to burden you. Now that you are stronger, it is time for you to know the truth."

Rachel clasped and unclasped her hands, her voice faltering. And although it was past midnight, she began her story.

She remembered returning to her family's apartment from the market and seeing a Nazi vehicle about to speed off. Her mother, father, husband and two young sons, Jurgen and Otto, were shackled in the back of the open truck, guarded by armed Nazi soldiers.

She remembered hearing the cries of the boys ... "Mamma ... Mamma ..." and seeing their outstretched arms and tear-stained faces as they caught sight of her.

She remembered that the lamb cutlets for the boys' dinner, which she'd bartered for in exchange for her mother's diamond ring at the marketplace that morning, were still in her bag.

She remembered that instinctively she ran behind the vehicle as it sped off. Her only thought was to be with her family and to comfort her children. Undetected by the Nazis and blind with grief she stumbled, falling down on the pavement with the provisions from her bag strewn about her.

But she did not remember how long she lay there.

It was Hans Grun who found her. Hans lived in the ground floor apartment beneath the one that Rachel shared with her family. He was the owner of a retail store selling men's suits; Rachel's father, Oskar, had owned a factory which manufactured menswear that he supplied to Hans's store. The two men had liked and respected each other, doing deals on a handshake. When Hitler's government passed a law prohibiting citizens from doing business with Jews, Oskar was forced to hand over his factory to the Germans.

Hans felt a profound sadness for the plight of the Jewish family living upstairs, and he shared his food rations with them whenever he could obtain a bit extra. Seeing Rachel lying on the pavement where she had fallen, her face and arms covered in blood, his heart surged with pity. He scrutinised the area to confirm that there were no soldiers about before he went to where Rachel lay, bruised and bleeding.

"Rachel, come with me before the Nazis return for you," he pleaded.

"Leave me here, Hans. I will wait for the Nazis to return for me. I would rather die than live without my family," murmured Rachel.

"*Liebchen*, what will another death help? Be strong for the sake of your family. Come with me," he coaxed.

With Hans's gentle but persistent persuasion, Rachel eventually allowed herself to be helped to her feet. She leant heavily on him as he led her to the safety of his apartment.

"Rachel, I have a small basement," he confided. "You can stay there until this terrible war is over."

"If the Nazis find me, Hans, we will both be shot. I cannot allow you to risk your life".

"Have faith, *Liebchen*, and trust me." Hans cleaned the blood off her face and then prepared a kettle of sweet, strong tea.

At night, when Hans felt it was safe, he would signal by

beating a broomstick against the floor and Rachel would emerge to share his rationed dinner with him. Rachel remained hidden in the basement until the war ended.

When the German army capitulated and the Allies arrived in Berlin, it was Rachel who protected Hans by revealing to the Allies how he had saved her life at great risk to his own.

In time, Hans Grun's name was honoured in Yad Vashem in Jerusalem in the Garden of the Righteous Among Nations.

Chapter 7

BERLIN

AUTUMN 1945

Helena kept her promise to Sofia to visit her in the military hospital where she remained under the care of Dr Luca. When Helena was able to complete her day's work at the administration office while it was still daylight, she would hurry along the pathway through the dense undergrowth that led to the hospital. She was anxious to return to the cottage before nightfall.

But one day was different.

Helena sat beside Sofia's hospital bed, holding her friend's hand and recounting tales of life in the cottage with Rachel and Max. Her heart lifted when Sofia clapped her hands in delight, charmed by the stories and enjoying Helena's company. So, Helena stayed just a bit longer.

By the time Helena wound her way home, dusk had faded into shades of purple. Shadows played menacingly across her path as night drew in. The cadence of the forest sounds settled ominously about her when she heard a voice haltingly call her name. She froze, her throat constricted with fear. Out of the shadows alongside the pathway, a figure emerged.

Max stepped out of the gloom of the tree-line pathway.

"Max! You startled me," she gasped as relief washed over her.

"Don't be afraid, Helena," Max said, gripping her shoulders to steady her as she stumbled against him. "I have been searching for you. Rachel and I were concerned when you had not yet returned and it was growing dark."

Helena leaned her head on Max's chest until her heart stopped racing. Then he slid his hand into hers, guiding her along the darkened pathway. She felt comforted by his protectiveness and the strength she recognised in him. In the calmness of Max's presence, she felt consoled. With a shared feeling of companionship, they made their way back towards the cottage.

Helena turned to Max.

"I know so little about you," she said. "Tell me about yourself, Max."

Max tightened his grip on Helena's hand and slowed his pace. In the intimacy of the night's stillness, in tranquil closeness, they exchanged their stories.

Max, the son of Russian immigrants Samuel and Yetta Harris, was raised in the Bronx in downtown New York before the family relocated to Manhattan. In 1920, Samuel and his brother Isaac had arrived in America, each bearing a battered brown leather suitcase containing their only possessions; little more than their prayer shawls and prayerbooks as well as a pair of their mother's silver wine goblets.

Samuel had left Yetta, his bride of a few months, behind in Russia, promising to send for her. His mother, with no daughters of her own, had given Yetta a pair of heavy silver candlesticks that had once belonged to her own mother. Later, when Samuel kept his promise and sent her a ticket to join him, Yetta carried these candlesticks with her to the shores of America.

When Samuel and Isaac Harris reached the Bronx, a fellow Russian who had arrived in America the previous year introduced them to Ethel Green, who ran a boarding house. Unlike many of the poor families who ran boarding houses out of necessity, Ethel did so by choice. She took an instant liking to the brothers and felt a genuine sympathy for them. Her youngest child had just left home, and she offered Samuel and Isaac the newly-vacated room for just a few dollars. Ethel would also provide an evening meal in exchange for help around the boarding house. Gratefully, Samuel and Isaac settled in, eager to repay Ethel's kindness.

Samuel's determination to send Yetta a ticket to join him saw the brothers set out each morning in search of employment. They pounded the dusty streets of a city clogged with people. The brothers would turn their hands to anything: shoe-shining or window cleaning, no job was too small. Every cent was scrupulously saved.

It was a swelteringly hot day when the brothers set out once more. The sun beat down, causing rivulets of sweat to trickle down their foreheads and pool in their necks beneath their collars. A dingy second-hand furniture store caught Samuel's attention. He wiped his brow with his shirt sleeve, and signalled to Isaac. The two men stepped into the coolness.

The owner, Charlie Miller, shuffled to the front of the store clutching his arthritic back. His bushy white eyebrows did not hide the kindness in his eyes. Introducing himself, he offered Samuel and Isaac refreshments. Over weak black tea in tall clear glasses, served with sugar lumps, they related their plight to an attentive Charlie, whose own success had been hard-earned.

Charlie Miller, together with his younger brother Danny, had spent his childhood in an orphanage and his adolescence foraging for food and shelter on the streets of New York. Charlie had only a shadowy memory of a mother and father. Their mother had died giving birth to Danny, and their father of a broken heart and poverty soon after. The young boys had been rescued by social workers and placed in care in an orphanage. When Charlie turned sixteen, it was time for him to leave the orphanage and Danny left with him.

As a means of survival for himself and his young brother, Charlie collected discarded bits of furniture. He had a gift for restoring them which he then re-sold. Eventually he was able to save enough money to open his own store. With the passage of time, and existing on the barest of necessities, Charlie scraped enough money together to send Danny to medical school. When Danny graduated as a surgeon and was posted to New York's Memorial Hospital, he and Charlie held on to each other and unashamedly shed tears. For these two brothers, the great American dream had been realised.

Charlie listened intently, identifying with the brothers' story. His brow was furrowed in thought. Eventually, steepling his hands beneath his chin, he said, "I need assistance. I will hire you both, but I can't pay much."

The brothers beamed. Overjoyed at the change in their fortunes Samuel and Isaac shook hands with Charlie, offering to start immediately.

A year later Samuel was able to purchase a passenger liner ticket for Yetta, and she arrived on Ellis Island to join him, bringing with her Samuel's mother's silver candlesticks. It was a jubilant occasion and the entire community celebrated her arrival until deep into the night.

Charlie had two daughters, Dee and Lilian. When they were growing up, Lilian was known as the pretty one and Dee as the more studious. With her thick lenses, neat plaits and serious disposition, the description fitted Dee well. It was Dee who invariably had her nose in a book while the more carefree Lilian romped about with the other kids in the neighbourhood. When Dee entered college, her life began to change and she became more self-assured. Her thirst for knowledge drew the attention of the lecturers, and her ability to prove mathematical theorems imbued her with a confidence she had lacked in her younger years.

Mark Stone was a young professor. In his tweed jacket and open-necked shirt, with his blond hair falling in a wave across his forehead, he cut a dashing figure. Dee, peering through her thick lenses, was drawn to him as were most of his female students. However, it seemed to her that his interest in her did not extend beyond DNA sequences and molecular biology. She assumed he regarded her as just another student whom he was willing to coach after classes.

It was the end of another day of lectures and the lecture hall had emptied, all but for Mark and Dee who were earnestly discussing scientific equations. Dee would have to leave for home soon. Wearily she removed her glasses, pressing her thumb and forefinger into the inner corners of her eyes. When she looked up Mark caught her gaze and was mesmerised. It seemed to him that Dee, without her glasses, was transformed. His eyes swept over her high, smooth forehead and strong jawline and he noticed the sparkle in her hazel eyes, usually concealed behind thick lenses.

Captivated, he leaned towards her.

"May I?" he asked softly.

Wordlessly she nodded and he gently tugged at her plaits, loosening them. Her thick chestnut hair fell in glinting waves, framing her face. Dee felt her heart thump against her ribcage. She blinked myopically at him as he gazed at her, absorbing every detail of the woman before him.

"Why, Dee," he exclaimed. "You are not only intelligent, but also quite beautiful."

Smiling demurely, Dee replaced her glasses and packed away her books. She sensed in that one heart-stopping moment that her friendship with Mark would become a much deeper one. It was to be an enduring relationship based on shared interests and mutual respect of each other's academic abilities.

It was the younger sister, Lilian, who caught Isaac's attention when the brothers visited the home of Charlie and his wife, Sarah, for sumptuous Sabbath suppers. Lilian's dancing brown eyes, her infectious smile and the bouncing curls that framed her face increasingly filled Isaac's thoughts. He quickly invented reasons to keep visiting the Miller home. Lilian eagerly awaited his visits. His quirky sense of humour and foreign accent fascinated her; besides, he was a fine, handsome man. As they spent more time together their friendship soon turned to romance.

On a steamy summer's night, under a lopsided moon, Isaac palmed back his hair and got down on one knee. In broken English, he asked his 'Leelian' to marry him. It was a magical night. Lilian had sensed Isaac's inner strength and she felt secure in his love; with eyes demurely downcast, she accepted his proposal.

An overjoyed Isaac approached Charlie to ask for his daughter's hand in marriage. Charlie would have preferred the older, more studious Dee to have married before her sister but seeing Lilian's face flushed with happiness, he blessed their union.

In the years that followed, the brothers and their families remained closely bonded with Charlie's family. Dee's academic aptitude led her to become a renowned scientist. She published highly-regarded research papers, and her close friendship with Mark Stone endured.

Isaac and Lilian's marriage was a happy and contented one. They raised two sons, Albie and Martin, who would with the passage of time be destined to control the family business, Miller Harris Furnishers.

Samuel and Isaac had a keen sense for business. Once they started working in Charlie's store, it began to thrive and soon their nightly meetings centred around plans for the opening of a second store. The business expanded rapidly, but so did Charlie's arthritis, and within a few years his rigid limbs rendered him unable to move about painlessly. Following the advice of Danny, he sold his share of the business to the Harris brothers who shrewdly continued to open more stores.

It was into this comfortable, middle-class environment and close-knit family that Max and his younger sister Gloria were born and raised.

After the defeat of Germany, news filtered out of Europe of the merciless efficiency of the German killing machine. Collective shockwaves reverberated around the world. The Harris family, stunned by the harrowing stories that were unfolding, put up no resistance when Max enlisted with Joint at the organisation's headquarters in New York and was sent to Berlin as a volunteer.

When Helena recounted the events of her life over the past few years, he slid an arm across her shoulders and drew her closer. In a pool of light cast by the moon breaking through the clouds, he turned to her. Looking deeply into her eyes, he searched for answers. Her answers caused him to lower his head as tears glistened on his lashes; His tears touched the pain deep within her. Cupping her face in his palms, hesitantly he brushed his lips against hers and felt the stirrings of a new emotion expanding in his chest.

So it happened that in the midst of the fear and uncertainty of her world and in spite of the madness that had been, Helena felt her heart open as she responded to Max's compassion. She was drawn to his decency and warmth. In turn, Max was captivated by the stoicism and dignity that radiated from her.

In the strangeness of this new reality, a love grew between Max and Helena; a love that would be severely tested in the uncertainty of the post-war years.

Chapter 8

BERLIN

WINTER 1945

Sofia rolls her wheelchair towards the glass panels of the solarium. A pale wintry sun filters through the glass, warming her skin. She yawns, stretches and hugs the rug spread across her knees closer to her. It has been many months since her arrival at the field hospital and the typhus still lingers. Despite many surgeries to her damaged feet, she is not yet able to walk. Dr Luca has transferred her to a convalescent home in Berlin where the dedicated nursing staff work tirelessly to restore her to good health.

She grows drowsy in the sun, her eyelids heavy. As she drifts into a gentle slumber, a shadow falls across her and the familiar voice of Dr Luca stirs her into wakefulness. He greets her, smiling kindly. Sofia's eyes are fixed on the white envelope he holds out to her. Her pulse quickens, and she looks at him questioningly.

He studies her closely.

"Do you know Nadia Treskye?" he asks.

It is as though a lightning bolt shoots through Sofia, the shock registering in her wide eyes. Gripping the sides of her wheelchair, she nods, "Yes," she says. The doctor looks at her questioningly and after a thoughtful pause she tells Dr Luca the circumstances that brought Nadia to her family home to become their housekeeper and to care for Sofia and her sister Anna. She describes how the motherly Nadia showed them unconditional love and, in turn, they nurtured a deep affection for her. Sofia remembers the sadness that overwhelmed her family when Nadia, forbidden to stay with them, disappeared from their lives.

As a young girl, Nadia could best be described as homely, but her gentle and loving nature drew people to her. She was the youngest of a family of seven children and her affection for her siblings was returned by each one. Their mother, Marta, had been widowed by the time Nadia turned two and the arduous burden of caring for her large family throughout the years took its toll, leaving Marta frail and fatigued.

One by one, Nadia's siblings left home as soon as they were able to fend for themselves. Most of them got married and produced numerous grandchildren for Marta. When the last of her siblings left home, Nadia found herself in the role of sole carer for Marta. Her soft heart would not allow her to abandon her mother. She remained at home and continued to tenderly take charge of her mother's needs, until the day Marta peacefully closed her eyes and drifted into oblivion, her journey on earth complete.

Nadia packed up the meagre possessions of the home she had shared with her mother and siblings. As she placed the photographs and memorabilia of a past life into wooden crates, Nadia came to acknowledge that she was past marriageable age and that anyway her plain looks would likely not attract suitors.

She came to accept that she would never hold her own babies in her arms or hear the sound of her children's laughter. She saw her life stretching empty and solitary before her.

For the first time she found herself entirely alone. Armed with only courage, she set out to obtain work that would provide her with independence. Mr Polanski, her neighbour, owned a grocery store. He told Nadia that one of his customers, Borzina Abrons, had asked him to help her find an honest and hardworking nursemaid for her two young daughters, Sofia and Anna.

Nadia was the perfect fit for the Abrons family. She had finally found her niche in the world and grew to love the two girls as though they were her own. She thrived in newfound happiness until the cataclysm of war struck the family and she was no longer allowed to work for Jews. Heartbroken, she was forced to leave the family she had grown close to.

Most of the surrounding towns were devastated by the ravages of war. Nadia moved away from the area and lost all contact with the Abrons family. In the aftermath of the war and as life settled down again in Poland, she set out to look for survivors of the family she had cared for so deeply.

Her search brought her to Joint and Dr Luca.

Sofia rips open the envelope and studies each word of the letter inside it. She reads of Nadia's joy at finding her and her offer to bring Sofia to Poland to live with her in her cottage in the countryside. Nadia says she has salvaged some of the Abrons family's possessions that the Nazis overlooked when looting their home, and she wishes to pass these on to Sofia.

Sofia had thought she would never see Nadia again, and the memory of her kindness mists her eyes and sparks a small flame of hope. Pensively, she considers Nadia's message to her.

The doctor weighs his words carefully.

"Sofia, I have done all I can for you. Arrangements have been made for you to travel to Poland, and Nadia will come to Berlin to help you with that journey. Are you willing to go?"

A flood of emotion engulfs Sofia. Dr Luca's reliability and his solidness have created a safe and trusting space in all the uncertainties of her life. Wordlessly, she nods her head.

The door of the solarium bursts open, bringing a gust of icy air as Helena, wrapped in a heavy army coat, rushes in. She has heard the news. She kneels in front of the wheelchair and folds Sofia in her arms, as though to hold the broken parts of her together. The doctor understands the immutable bond between the two women and is relieved that Helena is here to share this burden.

Before the war, Luca Rossi worked as a doctor in Florence, Italy, and when war was declared, he joined the Resistance. Working closely with Italian priests and cardinals, he was responsible for saving the lives of many Jews, especially children. He hid them in monasteries and cloisters where they could evade the Nazis until the war ended. Tragically, he had lost his only daughter to tuberculosis during an epidemic. Sofia brought back memories of his daughter and had endeared herself to him. Letting go of her wrenched at his heart.

Helena cups Sofia's face with her palms. Her tone is gentle but urgent.

"Sofia, it is time to go home and be safe."

"Come with me, Helena," Sofia implores.

"I must go to Palestine." A note of steely determination creeps into Helena's voice. "Together with the pioneers I will help build a country of our own, our home. Our children will never suffer as we have – never ever again."

Helena stands. "When I reach Palestine, I promise that I will send for you. Until then I will see you in the flame of my Sabbath candles and because of its spiritual light, we will always be connected."

With one last embrace, she turns to leave. The room shudders as the door slams shut.

Chapter 9

THE AMERICAN ZONE, BERLIN
WINTER, 1945

Palestine. It started as a whisper and had become a crescendo. It was the word on the lips of every refugee in the American Zone. It had become their desired destination. They no longer wished to return to their ruined homes and villages in Europe; they wanted a homeland of their own. They wanted to go to Palestine.

In the camp, emissaries worked among the refugees in an effort to help those dreams come true and to restore the displaced to a normal life. They worked secretly, trying to find ways of evading the British embargo that prevented Jews from reaching Palestine. The refugees attended meetings, hoping to be among a group selected to be smuggled out of Europe. Bowed shoulders became straighter and once-empty eyes began to flicker with hope. Reaching Palestine would provide them with the assurance that the genocide of their people could never happen again. *'Never Again'* became their mantra.

In her battle to survive, Helena had suppressed her emotions, but Max's gentleness reawakened her senses, helping her to heal and to feel again. The subtle changes that it brought to her had not gone unnoticed. Nor had it gone unnoticed that Max's smile lit up his face when Helena entered the room, or the tenderness with which he stroked her cheek with the back of his hand.

Rachel smiled inwardly when she noticed the colour rise, staining Helena's cheeks and the radiance that shone in her eyes when Max returned to the cottage at the end of the day. She observed the gentleness of the love that grew between Max and Helena, like the petals of a rosebud unfurling when touched by the warmth of the sun, and her heart was filled with contentment.

And yet ... Rachel sensed that Helena's experience in the camps had left her fragile and that healing would take time. She secretly worried for her young friend.

Evening has stroked the sky into shades of indigo blue when Helena sets out alone to the cottage. Her back aches from being hunched over the files all day in the office. The thought of sharing the day's events with Rachel and Max soothes her. So she quickens her pace.

In the cottage, she finds them seated at the wooden kitchen table, their heads bent close together in hushed conversation. Rachel's brow is creased with worry and Max's normally animated demeanour is solemn. Helena is filled with apprehension as she studies them. Max gestures to Helena and she sits facing him until at last he breaks the silence.

"My father has had a heart attack and I am needed back home in New York," he says gently, reaching for her hand. "I must leave immediately."

Helena sits frozen, her thoughts churning as she contemplates the vacuum Max will leave in her life, a life that has already been decimated by so much loss.

"Come with me. We can make our lives together in America," Max pleads, sensing her fragility.

Helena hesitates for just a moment before lifting her chin.

"Rachel and I are going to Palestine, however long it takes to get there. You need to go home, Max, but I need to follow my dream." She sees her apprehension reflected in his eyes.

Max looks defeated as he stands and folds her in his arms, holding her close to his heart.

"Then wait for me there, Helena. I promise that I will follow you as soon as I have cleared up matters at home. Please wait for me." His voice is muffled against her shoulder.

"The light of my Sabbath candles will keep us connected until we are together once more in Palestine. Their flame has lit my dark world and so have you," Helena answers, with a strangled sob.

An army truck rumbles up to the door of the cottage. The driver leaves the engine idling and calls to Max to hurry. Max slings his bag over his shoulder, ready to leave. Helena and Rachel walk towards the truck with him and he places his bag in the back. The driver signals to him and he hoists himself up onto the front seat. Despondently Helena and Rachel remain watching, their hands raised in farewell, as the truck lumbers off, coating them in a cloud of fine dust. Rachel tucks Helena protectively under her arm as they return to the cottage.

It feels as though all the colour has drained from their world.

The weeks that followed his departure left Helena with an aching sense of loss.

It felt to her as though time had been suspended. She abandoned herself to working long and exhausting hours in the office to keep Max from occupying all her thoughts, but memories of him tugged endlessly at her. She conjured up his features; his lopsided smile and the quirk of his eyebrow. She recalled their shared confidences and the touch of his hand on hers. His letters from New York were eagerly awaited and she and Rachel poured over every word.

Meanwhile, the two women continued to hope that they would eventually find a way of reaching Palestine.

The night air was crisp, turning Helena's breath to fog as she left the administration office at the end of the day. As she neared the cottage, an army Jeep drew up alongside her and a young soldier hopped out, thrusting an envelope at her.

"Are you Helena? My instructions are to hand this to you. Please report to the Main Administration Block tomorrow at 7am." Deftly he hoisted himself back into the Jeep and with a quick salute sped off.

She tore open the envelope, her eyes hungrily scanning the handwritten letter inside it. As she absorbed the contents she became aware that her life was about to change once again.

The following morning, lingering grey clouds drifted across a leaden sky as Helena strode towards the Administration Block, her shoulders hunched against the cold. She lifted the collar of her ill-fitting army coat and pulled the knitted beanie lower over her forehead. Her hair was beginning to grow and was now long enough to tuck a loose blonde wisp behind her ear. Sweeping gusts of wind billowed around her. The message she received from the soldier had left her unsettled, with her thoughts in turmoil. She wrapped her arms tightly across her chest.

The enticing aroma of coffee filled the air as she entered the office. A soldier stood watch over a steaming percolator. The room was austerely furnished, the only dim light provided by a naked overhead globe. Herbie Feldman, a senior Joint official, appeared from an inner office. He was a burly man with a heavy beard and perceptive eyes. With a fluid motion, he offered her coffee and a seat. Warmed by the mug of scalding coffee and Herbie's friendly smile, she felt her tension ease.

He repeated the message that was delivered to her by the soldier the night before, filling in details.

Her only surviving relatives, her mother's brother Jacques Blum and his wife Amelie, had been located in Paris. Aware of her plight and her need to reach Palestine, they had offered to arrange passage for Helena and Rachel to Paris. They would accommodate them in their home until arrangements could be made for their journey on to Palestine.

Helena's grandparents, Mendel and Sheina Blum, had emigrated to Palestine from Poland before the war. Both had beseeched Tateh and Mameh to follow them, or at least to allow Helena and Eva to do so. But Tateh was steadfast in his refusal.

However, the knowledge that her grandparents were safe in Palestine and the thought that she could be reunited with them, had provided her with a small glimmer of hope.

Now hearing Herbie speak of her only surviving relatives living in Paris, a sense of dread overwhelmed Helena. She returned Herbie's direct gaze and implored him, "Where are my grandparents?"

"They have both passed away," he answered, gently entering into the aura of her sorrow.

"But Helena, this time you will have graves to visit and a place to feel spiritually connected to your grandparents. I hope that this will bring you a measure of comfort."

Helena's heart clenched with grief. She would have to come to terms with yet another loss, that of her beloved Bubbe and Zayde, as well as the loss of hope which she had unwaveringly clung to, that they would be reunited in Palestine.

Herbie felt profound compassion for this young woman, little more than a girl, who sat before him. Taking both her hands in his, he gave the account of how the Blum family had survived the Nazi occupation of Paris.

Soon after the Germans invaded Paris, the round-up of Jews began in earnest. No one doubted where these Jews were headed. Cattle trucks tightly packed with Jews and immigrants, the elderly and infirm, children, men and women were being sent to the death camps of Poland and Germany.

Jacques Blum was a member of the Underground and had close ties with Father Francis, a priest who had helped many

Jews cross the border safely into Switzerland. Jacques appealed to him to keep his young daughters, Celeste and Violetta, safe in a cloister so that he and Amelie could take refuge in Nice while working with the Resistance.

Under cover of night, frightened and distraught at being separated from their parents, the two girls were delivered to Sister Madeleine, the Mother Superior of a nearby cloister. The stern-looking nun asked no questions but welcomed them and introduced them to the other girls in the dormitory, many of whom were also in hiding.

The following morning, Sister Agnes placed towels about the shoulders of Celeste and Violetta and set about cutting off their thick, dark plaits. Then she lightened their hair with a strong-smelling dye. A kind-hearted woman, she understood the girls' despair at losing their long hair but comforted them by explaining that it was for their protection. With their lightened hair they were now indistinguishable from the other, French Catholic, girls. In the following days they were taught the Lord's Prayer and made to recite it until they could do so without any prompting.

The Nazis were known to raid cloisters in the dead of night without warning, aiming to seek out Jewish girls. If the girls were able to recite the Lord's Prayer, the Nazis would accept that they were indeed Catholic. Once the soldiers left, the girls would return to their dormitories tired and confused, while the relief of the nuns was palpable.

After the defeat of Germany and the retreat of the Nazis from Paris, the Blums returned to the cloister, anxious to be reunited with their daughters. Joyous tears were shed as Jacques and Amelie scooped the girls into their arms. Displaying her gratitude, Amelie clasped Sister Madeleine's hands. She acknowledged that although she would never be able to repay the nuns for their kindness to her daughters, she would continue to visit the cloister to assist them and contribute to their charities.

The names of Father Francis and Sister Madeleine were among those displayed in Yad Vashem after the war, once the State of Israel had been declared.

Jacques and Amelie and their daughters returned to Paris to find their home reasonably intact, but Paris was a city with a broken heart. Throughout the city, billboards and lampposts carried names and descriptions of missing people: Henri, eight years old and wears glasses; Colette has blonde curls and sucks her thumb ... These were among the notices placed by broken-hearted parents who had returned from the camps.

The summer wind dried the parents' tears and swept away their last vestiges of hope as the city returned to its business.

Herbie Feldman placed a comforting hand on Helena's shoulder. "It is good you have a home to go to, Helena. It is time for you to start a new life."

Helena felt her heart beat like a trapped bird as it dawned on her that she would be leaving Germany. "I will not go without Rachel," she answered defiantly.

"Rachel will travel with you. Arrangements have been made," Herbie placated her. Helena nodded her acceptance and, having drained her coffee, stood to leave.

Herbie folded her into his bearlike arms. "God speed little one. You have been a treasure to all of us in the office." Just for a moment, Helena nestled in the safety of his embrace before stepping out into the biting winter wind.

The following weeks were filled with frenzied planning. Paperwork had to be processed and completed before train tickets could be issued for Rachel and Helena's journey to Paris. Correspondence between Jacques and Helena helped pave the way for their new home in Paris and Rachel and Helena eagerly awaited these letters. Helena was disappointed that her cousins Violetta and Celeste were being sent to school in America and that she would not yet meet them in Paris.

Finally, the arrangements were concluded. The two women prepared to depart from the American Zone and to leave behind the residents with whom they have formed close relationships. With a mixture of sadness and anticipation Helena and Rachel said their last goodbyes.

A tentative spring had melted away the last of the winter snow as Rachel closed the cottage door for the last time. Green shoots bravely appeared on branches that had been stripped bare by an unforgiving winter, and birdsong once again filled the air.

A soldier in an army Jeep was waiting outside the cottage to transfer them to the train station. When they appeared, he honked the hooter and hopped out to open the Jeep's door. Helena hesitated for just a moment. She turned to look back at the cottage where she had felt anchored and in which she was cocooned by the love of Rachel and Max. Now, only uncertainty stretched before her. But Rachel was Helena's North Star and having her by her side emboldened her. Their arms entwined, the two women walked towards the waiting Jeep.

Rachel and Helena sat side by side on the station platform bench waiting for the arrival of the train that would carry them to Paris. Their rucksacks were at their feet. The shrillness of the guard's whistle and the pulsating energy of travellers rushing onto the platform swamped the air with sound.

A dusty train lurched into the station, its screeching wheels adding to the deafening noise. The doors of the carriages swung open. Selecting the one closest to them, Helena and Rachel settled onto the comfortable leather seats, only dimly aware of their fellow travellers.

Rachel turned to Helena with a triumphant smile. "*Schatzi,* we are leaving Germany. The war is over, and we have survived."

Helena slipped her arm through Rachel's and rested her head on her shoulder.

The train shunted out of the station, leaving behind a trail of blue-grey smoke. Only as they peered through the train window and observed the changing names of the stations through which the train passed, could they fully accept that they were finally leaving Germany. The savage crimes of war they had witnessed in the concentration camps were in the past. In the rumbling wheels of the train, they heard a repeated refrain: '*You-are-free, you-are-free*' it called tantalisingly back at them.

As the train hurtled along the track, Rachel drifted off to sleep with her chin resting on her chest. Helena, lulled by the rocking carriage, leaned her head against the back of the leather seat as the monotonous clatter of the wheels evoked dreamlike memories. The shadowy forms of ghosts from her past invaded her reverie, mingling with images of Sofia and Max, as though time was unspooling the years of her life. Closing her eyes, she could see Sofia's face imprinted on the back of her eyelids. It brought her comfort to know that Sofia was back in Poland and being cared for by Nadia in her country cottage.

After the war there had been an uprising in Poland. Once the Russians invaded and the Communists took control, life had become precarious and again there were shortages of food and medical supplies. Despite these new uncertainties, Nadia took care of Sofia as gently as she would an infant. She bathed her, braided her hair and massaged her feet, encouraging her, futilely, to take a few steps. Her cottage provided a haven for Sofia. Vegetables grew abundantly in Nadia's tiny garden, and her cooking and the country air brought some colour to Sofia's cheeks. But there was no cure for the heinous crimes that had been inflicted on her.

Sofia's letters reached Helena regularly, filled with news of her life back in Poland and Nadia's kindness. Still, Helena sensed the deep feeling of loss and solitude that haunted Sofia, hindering her recovery.

At the beginning of each Sabbath, when the sun dipped over the horizon, Sofia and Helena both lit their Sabbath candles.

In the flickering flames they each mouthed a silent prayer, and felt connected despite the vast distance between them.

Max's letters became less frequent as time passed, which clouded Helena's heart with sadness. Max had been her bridge from hopelessness to the possibility of being happy again. She clung resolutely to the belief that he would fulfil his promise to meet her in Palestine.

Chapter 10

PARIS

SPRING 1946

It was dusk as the train shuddered to a halt, jolting Helena into wakefulness and rousing her from her dreams. Rachel was still asleep, her head resting on Helena's shoulder, her mouth slightly ajar. Helena nudged her and her eyes flickered open. A rush of cold air entered the carriage as the doors swung open, disgorging passengers who spilled out onto the platform waving and calling excitedly to the milling throng who were there to meet them.

Rachel and Helena were dressed in the Polish officers' uniforms that they had been given to wear to safely cross the border into France. They stood expectantly among the jostling crowd, clutching their rucksacks while scrutinizing the people for anyone appearing to meet them. A short rotund figure weaved through the congested platform towards them.

Jacques Blum had a broad, generous face and lips that curled into a ready smile.

"Rachel? Helena?" he asked, arms outstretched, although there was no doubt in his mind that these two oddly-dressed women were his charges.

Folding Helena into a bear hug, he studied her intently, his eyes misting as he noted the resemblance to his sister, Helena's mother. He had been told by a survivor from the camp where his sister had been taken, that she had walked bravely, with her head held high, into the gas chambers.

Jacques greeted Rachel warmly too, taking both her hands into his. Then he hoisted the two rucksacks onto his shoulder and ushered the women out of the station towards his vehicle.

Dusk had faded into darkness and stars pricked the sky as Jacques drove up to the Blum's apartment. Amelie was waiting for them in the open doorway. She was slightly taller than her husband, a startlingly beautiful woman. Her dark hair, rolled back severely into a fashionable chignon, emphasised her chiselled features. She air-kissed Helena and Rachel on both cheeks.

Holding them at arm's length, she studied the clothes they were wearing and, with twinkling eyes and a prominent French accent, announced: "Tomorrow we go shopping."

The Blums welcomed Helena and Rachel into their home. Although they had never met until that day, their experiences drew them together to bond as a family. The Blums' two daughters had left home to study at a school in America. The large apartment with its wide-open rooms had felt strangely lonely with only the footsteps of Jacques and Amelie to echo eerily in the empty halls. They looked forward to the companionship of Helena and Rachel.

When Amelie was eight years old, Maman packed her meagre belongings into a brown paper bag and dropped Amelie and the bag off at her sister's house.

"Your Maman has gone in search of your Papa, and she will

come back for you once she has found him," said her aunt, not caring much about the matter one way or the other.

But Amelie never saw her Maman again.

Her aunt shuffled about all day in worn-out slippers, a lit cigarette dangling between her nicotine-stained fingers, leaving Amelie to fend for herself most of the time.

Amelie never knew her Papa. When she ran around the backstreets of Pigalle with the other urchin children, she imagined that every strong, handsome man she saw might be her Papa. She dreamed that Maman and Papa would come for her, but they never did.

She learned to deal with the loss that left an empty space deep within her. When she was sixteen her aunt died, leaving her penniless and alone, and she gave up pretending to the other children that she had a real family. However hard she tried to recall Maman's face, it had become blurred. She would, however, always remember the feel of her skin and the smell of her hair when she hugged Amelie for the last time. Now she was left to fend for herself by foraging on the streets of Paris. But beneath the ragged dress she wore, regardless of her unwashed hair and grime-streaked face, a beauty was emerging. Amelie had grown tall and lean, and moved with the grace of a young colt.

Each afternoon the tinkling notes of a piano drifted across the noise of the traffic, the congestion of pedestrians hurrying about their business, and hawkers calling out their wares. Amelie was enchanted by the music and one afternoon she followed the sound to a low white building with windows reaching almost to the pavement. She flattened her forehead against the glass, her hands on either side of her face, and peered inside. Young girls wearing pink tights and tutus were practising ballet steps, holding on to a side barre. It was the soft pink ballet slippers they wore that Amelie most desired. The instructor stood in front of them, tapping out the tempo of the music against the floor with the long cane she held. She was dressed in a black tutu and leotard and her hair was scraped back into a bun covered with a snood at the nape of her neck.

Amelie was enthralled with the music and the ballet scenes she witnessed. She returned every afternoon to watch closely as the children practised the steps. Undetected, she emulated the ballet steps until she learned to dance. Then she danced for the urchins on the street and before long, fascinated bystanders were throwing pennies at her when she danced for them.

He wore a pinstriped suit and a white bowler hat and there was always a cigar protruding between his thick lips, this man who came to watch her dance on the street corner every day. Then, early one morning, he came looking for her. He smiled at her, revealing a gold tooth in the front of his mouth, and offered to buy her a meal at the best restaurant in Pigalle. The urchin child was beguiled by him and by the prospect of a good meal, and she trustingly put her hand in his. Amos was his name and he became her Big Papa.

Amos bought her new clothes and then took her to his apartment where she was immersed in a deep, pink bathtub filled with perfumed water. She emerged from the tub clean and naked, and Amos said, "Dance for me". So she did.

Out of the dirt and grime of the backstreets of Paris, a new Amelie was emerging. She learned that her body could provide her with the love and security that she yearned for in the same way that her dancing had provided her with pennies for her survival.

Amos owned a dance hall in Pigalle and he set Amelie up dancing there at night. She wore a glittering two-piece costume, with a high feathered headdress placed on her head. Her long, lithe body and the thick dark hair cascading down her back dazzled the men in the audience. They tucked folded bills into her costume and vied for her attention. But she was Amos's girl, and Amos knew how to treat a lady. He showered her with gifts of jewellery and expensive perfume. She spent hours shopping in the boutiques of the Champs-Élysées where she was fawned over by the assistants.

Maître d's bowed to greet her as they scraped back her chair at the best table in the restaurant and fluttered white linen napkins across her lap.

Jacques Blum was a final-year student at the Sorbonne. Known to his peers as Jacques, he had arrived in Paris from a small Polish town as Jacob Blum. Jacob was the youngest of five siblings and the only son of Mendel and Sheina Blum. From a young age Jacob was perpetually armed with a notebook and pencil, sketching every shape and form that his artistic eye perceived. His four sisters pampered their young brother and indulged his fantasies of a career constructing modern, high-rise buildings once he had completed his schooling. When Jacob entered higher grades at school, his artistic gift gained the attention of his instructors. In his final year, he was awarded a scholarship to study at the architectural school at the Sorbonne in Paris, renowned for its high standard of excellence.

When it was time for him to leave home, his proud family accompanied him to the train station. Tearfully, Mendel had blessed his only son before he left their home, and at the train station, his sisters held him close. Sheina had prepared a parcel of food to sustain him on his journey. It contained pierogi, Zurek soup, cabbage rolls and fresh fruit.

"Please remember to honour the Sabbath while you are away from home," she implored Jacob, gathering him into her arms.

Jacob looked stricken as he bade his devoted family one last farewell. Then, with the worn leather suitcase in one hand and the food parcel tucked beneath his other arm, he boarded the train that would take him to Paris to begin a new chapter and fulfil his childhood dreams.

"He is still so young," sighed Sheina as the train chugged out of the station.

"He has a good head on his shoulders. I trust him to make the right decisions." Mendel nodded sagely.

In the aftermath of the war in Europe, a war that was yet to be waged, Jacob would have the comfort of knowing that Sheina and Mendel had evaded the death camps. They had left Poland at the first sign of the approaching war to settle in Palestine and so had survived the war, only to die of natural causes soon after.

Jacob never got to see his sisters again. All four had married and decided to remain in Poland with their respective families; all four were slaughtered in Nazi concentration camps.

Jacques was enjoying a raucous night of carefree drinking with fellow students. It was late and they were already tipsy when they decided to pay a visit to Amos's infamous dance hall instead of heading back to the Sorbonne.

The first time Jacques saw Amelie she was gliding across the floor and he felt as though he had fallen off the edge of the world. He was mesmerised by her beauty.

Sobering up, he attempted to invite her over to his table for a drink but she rejected all his advances. He was captivated by this elusive woman and began to pursue her relentlessly, visiting the dance hall nightly. But Amelie refused to accept any of the invitations offered by this eager, clean-shaven young student. She belonged to Papa Amos and she made it known.

Then, in one night of violence, like the twist of a kaleidoscope, the pattern of Amelie's life changed again. Gunmen burst into the dance hall shooting randomly as patrons screamed and ran for cover. The gunmen wanted Amos, who owed their boss money – lots of it, and they were there to collect. When they found Amos cowering under a table they stabbed him, then they emptied the tills and left. Amos was rushed to hospital with the knife still protruding from his torso, but the mob boss's mission was accomplished and Amos did not survive.

When the dance hall was locked up Amelie's world came crashing down, and she once again found herself alone on the streets of Paris.

Returning to the dance hall and finding it closed Jacques was crestfallen at the thought of losing Amelie. Each evening after lectures, he scoured the streets of Pigalle in search of her. It seemed as though she had disappeared into thin air.

Then one evening, hungry and deflated, he was about to return to the Sorbonne when the smell of chocolate crepes being cooked on an open brassiere drifted towards him.

He approached the chef who was dressed in a tall white chef's hat and enveloped in a wrap-around apron. While waiting for the crepes he'd purchased, he enquired about Amelie.

"Oh yes" replied the chef, deftly tossing a crepe into the air and back in the pan. "I know the lady you are looking for. She lives on the top floor of the rooming house behind you."

Thanking the chef, Jacques climbed the rickety staircase leading to Amelie's room.

"Let me help you, Amelie," he coaxed the reclining figure wrapped in a yellowing sheet on a sunken mattress in an airless room.

This time she did not reject his offer. She saw something in him that she began to trust, and he guided her through the chaos of her life. He assisted her in finding employment in the cosmetic section of a department store. A year later, when Jacques had qualified with honours as an architect, they were married quietly in a civil ceremony.

Amelie shed her past life as an urchin dancing in the backstreets of Paris for pennies as completely and permanently as a ladybird sheds its outer shell. She emerged as Madame Blum, the wife of a prosperous businessman, living a comfortable life on the Rue des Rosiers.

When Rachel and Helena arrived at her home, survivors of the horrific crimes that had taken place in Europe, Amelie recognised the unbearable loss imprinted in the slope of their shoulders and in the pain in their eyes. She was transported back to her own troubled past, the memories of which remained deeply buried within her, and she opened her heart as well as her home to the two fragile women.

Chapter 11

PARIS

SUMMER 1946

Over countless cups of coffee enjoyed around the kitchen table, Amelie and Rachel exchanged recipes. Rachel prepared traditional German meatballs in a white sauce while Amelie introduced her to French cuisine – and French fashion. Rachel allowed Amelie to style her hair and she exchanged her shapeless shift dress for one of Amelie's latest designs. She stared into the mirror in wide-eyed amazement as she saw herself transformed. Amelie smiled secretly as she heard Rachel humming while she dusted and swept around the apartment. She would make believe that the broom was a dancing partner with which she tried out the latest steps to the music coming from the radio.

In a quiet moment, Jacques drew Helena into his wood-panelled study. It was lined with book-filled shelves. Unshuttered windows allowed the summer sunlight to flood the room, bathing it in a mellow ambience. As the evenings and the months grew cooler Jacques would light the embers in the hearth and they would crackle and sigh as they warmed the room. The study would become a safe and trusting space for Helena in which she and Jacques would share many significant discussions.

Sitting across from Jacques in a softly-padded, well-worn

armchair, she listened attentively as he confirmed the passing of his parents, her Bubbe and Zayde, Sheina and Mendel. She dabbed at her eyes with the handkerchief crushed in her palm and soaked with her tears.

Jacques described the last years of the elderly couple's lives, emphasising that they had adapted well to their new home and had made many friends among the pioneers with whom they worked the land. Both died of old age, perhaps facilitated by the harsh conditions of a new country, but they had passed peacefully, in their sleep, and within weeks of each other.

Helena gazed up at Jacques. She had lost her beloved grand-parents with whom she had hoped to be reunited, but it dawned on her that she had found a new family and a loving uncle.

Pierre Lamont was a friend of Jacques' who owned a millinery factory called Pompadour. His factory had survived the war and continued to expand and there was a vacancy for a machinist. He offered the position to Helena. When Jacques conveyed Pierre's offer to her, a tremor of apprehension passed down her spine and she took deep, steadying breaths until the pounding in her chest subsided. The idea of integrating back into a functioning community left her feeling vulnerable and afraid. And yet, she sensed, employment would provide her with a feeling of worth and she would gain her independence. So she bravely decided to embrace the opportunity being offered to her.

The following morning, she dressed with care. She chose to wear the soft lilac skirt and dove-grey blouse with shiny pearl buttons down the back and on the cuff that Amelie had picked out for her. She was confident of Amelie's fashion sense. Her narrow waist was cinched with a wide, white belt and Amelie brushed Helena's hair until it shone. It was decided that Jacques would accompany Helena to Pompadour to introduce her to Pierre and to the women with whom she would work.

Helena pulsed with nervous excitement. At first, she refused the breakfast of cinnamon pancakes filled with fresh berries that Rachel had prepared for her. Then, with coaxing from Rachel and Amelie, she tried one pancake and then asked for another. Jacques gulped down a mug of coffee, wiped his mouth with the back of his hand, and announced that it was time to leave for Pompadour. Amelie and Rachel sensed Helena's hesitancy and hugged her reassuringly as she left with Jacques.

It was a perfect summer day. Helena threaded her arm through Jacques' as they set out. The early morning rays of the sun warmed their skin and had a calming effect on Helena. When they arrived at Pompadour, Pierre welcomed Helena. He led her around the factory, introducing her to her fellow machinists. He demonstrated how the hats were produced and indicated what functions would be required of her.

Hats were an important fashion accessory that summer. Helena was fascinated with the world that was revealed to her while working in Pierre's factory. She proved to be as adept at creating new styles as she was at using a sewing machine. Bolts of opulent fabrics were transformed into headpieces of all shapes: deep velvets, sumptuous silks in jewel shades, and emerald- and amethyst-coloured ribbons became wide-brimmed feathered hats or close-fitting cloches. Pierre Lamont noted that it was Helena's creations that were the most sought-after by the elegant women of Paris. He was intrigued with this slim, shy girl with the veiled expression and abundant talent, and watched over her protectively.

It became evident to Helena that it was essential that she master the French language, so she enrolled at night school. She had lost her final years of schooling in Poland to the war and she was determined to complete her education.

When she arrived home from college, and after dinner, she would laboriously pour over the homework given to her. She encouraged Rachel to follow her example and become conversant in French. The two women studied together, spending hours forming the sounds that were so new to their ears. Mostly they would dissolve into spluttering fits of laughter but to the surprise of Amelie and Jacques, they were soon conversing in French with ease.

After dinner in the evenings that Helena did not attend college, she and Rachel listened closely to Jacques as he recounted the details of what happened in Paris during the war years.

Germany invaded France in May 1940 and, after brief initial resistance, the French army capitulated. Although factories and working-class suburbs were heavily bombed, Paris was left virtually unscathed and art and culture flourished.

The American author Gertrude Stein had turned her home in Paris into a salon for artists, writers and poets. Pablo Picasso, Henri Matisse, Ernest Hemingway and Ezra Pound were among her frequent visitors. Herself a Jew, Gertrude Stein was protected by the German sympathisers, Philippe Pétain and Bernard Fay, whom she admired.

Food was still scarce after the war, but there was a flourishing black market through which essential items were obtainable. Most Parisian institutions recovered quickly. In early 1946, the first major fashion show was held by Christian Dior. High fashion thrived and Coco Chanel became a fashion icon with her creation of the trouser suit for women. The motor car industry revived and put on a glittering show in the same year.

On the days she didn't work at Pompadour, Helena strolled along the steamy streets and boulevards of summertime Paris. Post-war Paris was flush with art and culture, ablaze with vibrant colour, and Helena revelled in all it had to offer. Brightly striped umbrellas adorned every sidewalk café. She admired the fashionably-dressed men and women who sat beneath them, languidly sipping frothy lattes and nibbling fresh patisseries. She mingled with young lovers who ambled hand in hand beside the Seine, watching tugboats chugging along the silvery river that shimmered in the summer heat.

In the artists' colony, scenes of Paris came alive as artists in paint-splattered smocks dabbed more paint on canvasses stacked on easels. Poets recited their poetry on street corners and in salons, where sophisticated thinkers also congregated to enthusiastically debate their new ideas. Music from carousels saturated the air, blending with the laughter of children who skipped alongside their rolling hoops. Helena embraced Paris and all of its beauty. The sun had warmed the heart of Paris and she basked in its warmth.

A metamorphosis was happening to Helena and she relished the sensation of just being alive. But still, the flimsiness of her happiness could be fragmented by the tender innocence of a sound, a touch or a smell evoking memories so powerful that she felt as though she was being reeled back in time to the camp.

The aroma of freshly baked bread rose into the air as she strolled past a corner bakery on her way home. The reminiscence it triggered caused her heart to beat wildly and she staggered towards a nearby railing to brace herself against it.

In the clarity of the vision before her, she recalled her days in the labour camp where she was one of a small group of women who pushed carts filled with stones endlessly and needlessly along highways and roads.

The smell of bread emanating from the kitchen of a nearby bakery drifted towards them. The women, hungry and exhausted, were crazed by the smell of fresh bread and fell upon the bakery begging for bread.

All but Helena. She stood aside, guarding her cart of stones. All she had left was her dignity and she clung to it. Although hunger gnawed at her, she would not beg. She remained behind the group, tears spilling silently down her cheeks. How she longed for the bread the other women were bound to receive. In the midst of the hopelessness that engulfed her, she heard a voice calling her name and felt a hand prod her shoulder. Turning in alarm, she stared bewilderedly into the face of Michal, a school friend from her hometown.

"Why are you here, Michal?"

"I have been sent by the Nazis to work in this bakery. I saw you crying and slipped this out for you," he whispered, glancing over his shoulder to make sure there were no guards watching. Then he thrust a loaf of hot bread into her open palms.

"Leave now," he urged, before disappearing towards the back door of the bakery.

Helena hid the bread in her clothing and lifted her stone-filled cart with renewed energy. There was a sense of lightness about her as she joined the group of women, knowing that the bread would provide a feast for all of them that night.

Helena regained her composure as the vision faded and her racing pulse began to slow. The memories of all that she endured, and the promise that she'd made to Max and Sofia, strengthened her resolve to keep seeking a passage to Palestine for Rachel and herself.

But no-one could have predicted the events that were unfolding in the Middle East.

Chapter 12

PARIS
1946-1947

Helena and Rachel were adjusting to the ebb and flow and familiarity of life with Jacques and Amelie as the days spiralled into weeks and then months. Jacques was well connected to underground organisations such as Bricha; the name Bricha meaning 'flight', that aided Jewish survivors fleeing war-ravaged Europe. But there were punitive regulations strictly enforced by the British, who controlled Palestine. Many ships, like the Exodus, were intercepted and tens of thousands of survivors on board were herded to holding camps in Cyprus.

In Paris, spring had melted away the iciness of winter as the Passover festival was ushered in. The scent of apple blossom wafted in the still evening air. Goblets of sweet red wine were raised, and 'Next year in Jerusalem' was the murmured refrain around the table. The preparation for this festival had brought an aching reminder to both Rachel and Helena of the festivals celebrated in their own homes before the war, the Passover festival being the most poignant. The crisp white table linen and the fragrant aroma that arose from platters of roasted meat, herbed fishes and French-fried potatoes reminded Helena of all she had lost and the childhood that was stolen from her.

The memory of the last Passover she shared with her family on Polna Street overwhelms her thoughts. The image becomes so vivid that the faces of the people seated around the table seem to blur and fade, replaced with those of her grandfather, grandmother, father, mother and Eva.

Their conversation so clearly remembered echoes about her. Voices that are lost in the past.

"Rudi." Her grandfather Mendel said leaning earnestly towards Tateh and nervously stroking his own heavy beard. "The war-noises grow louder every day, as does the hatred of the Jews. It is time to leave Poland. Your mother-in-law and I are leaving for Palestine within a few weeks. Please, Rudi, you should all come along with us."

"Tateh," replied Rudi. "I do not believe that there will be a war. Besides, I am Polish and this is my country. I have all I need right here."

"Son," urged grandmother Sheina, "If you and your wife won't leave, then please allow us to take Helena and Eva with us to Palestine."

"No Mameh, our children have all their comforts here and we will not be separated from them." Rudi's voice was stern, holding up both his hands to indicate the end of the conversation.

Slowly the image dissolves as Helena returns to the present and is drawn back into the chatter flowing around the table. The meal ends once the imaginary Elijah has been welcomed and grace recited.

Jacques retired to his study, signalling to Helena to join him.

When she entered the study, he was reclining in his favourite armchair in front of the smouldering coals in the hearth. In the glow, she saw the anxiety reflected in his eyes as he drew up a chair for her beside him.

"Lenie," he called her by her childhood name. "You and Rachel will need to be patient for a while longer. The British have increased their restrictions on refugees entering Palestine and the whole area is in upheaval with the region being on the brink of war. I do not want you to risk going with Bricha, because if you get caught you could be sent to Cyprus. The camps there are overcrowded and the conditions inhumane. Therefore, I am investigating every other possible way for you and Rachel to reach Palestine safely."

"I know." Helena said, bending to kiss the top of his head. "You have opened your heart and your home to Rachel and me, and I do not expect more from you."

"In your eyes, I see my mother."

Standing up to leave, she faltered for just a moment. "Sleep well uncle," she said, closing the door gently behind her.

Chapter 13

NEW YORK

1945-1947

Samuel Harris's ailing heart held out until Max returned home from Berlin. Since first arriving on American soil so many years ago, Samuel had worked relentlessly to create the success of Miller Harris Furnishers, which now comprised thirty-two stores spread throughout New York. As Samuel's last breath floated away from him, his distraught family huddled around his bedside, detected a smile of satisfaction tugging at the corners of his mouth. They too smiled through their tears as they prepared for a week of mourning.

Max struggled to adjust to his new surroundings. The disparity of the lavishness of his home compared to the poverty and despair of the survivors in Berlin filled him with sadness. However, the gap caused by Samuel's death and the deep sorrow that it caused could not be ignored, and he felt the burden of assuming the role of head of the family.

Isaac Harris had continued to play an active role in the business of Miller Harris Furnishers, but he had become stooped with years of work and worry. His sons Albie and Martin, and Max's sister Gloria, attended to the bulk of the business. Throughout the passing years the sisters-in-law Yetta and Lilian had developed a close relationship, made more so by their mutual pleasure in preparing traditional dishes and large meals for their expanding family.

Gloria had morphed from a pimply teenager into an exotic beauty. Her doe-shaped hazel eyes and translucent complexion was offset by a mane of luxuriant dark hair which swept her shoulders and drew many admiring glances. A deep dimple appeared in her cheek whenever she smiled which she did often, displaying perfect white teeth.

Yetta was proud of her beautiful daughter. She fussed over her, grooming her for Gloria's coming out party as a debutante.

Gloria had a well-stocked wardrobe of designer frocks and regularly visited the beauty parlour. Her diary was filled with social engagements. It was at a charity ball that she first caught the eye of Daniel Jonas, a Wall Street banker. She was wearing a creation of white and silver satin that emphasised her statuesque figure and bared one smooth shoulder.

While Gloria was holding sway over a bevy of admirers, Daniel first spotted her and he was determined that he would make her his wife. But Gloria was young, and he accepted that he would have to bide his time and be cautious in his pursuit. However, within a year he had swept Gloria off her feet and she married him. The marriage produced two sons, both of whom inherited their mother's good looks, but it was doomed to fail.

The closeness Max and Gloria shared as children continued into their adult lives. Max adored his sister and was fiercely protective of her. The many suitors who called at the Harris home were meticulously scrutinised by him, and Gloria respected his judgement. Max felt uneasy when he first met the handsome, successful and controlling Daniel Jonas and he conveyed his feelings to a besotted Gloria, but she was determined to marry the man she professed to love.

Daniel Jonas was as smart as a whip. He was also very ambitious. Once he had acquired a beautiful wife to display on his arm and arouse the envy of his colleagues, he set his sights on the corporate ladder and his rise was meteoric. The hours he spent at the office became longer as Gloria's life grew lonelier. Most nights he slept on a daybed in his office, claiming that the two boisterous young boys at home prevented him from giving the necessary attention to the workload in his study. He preferred the solitude of his office and seemed impervious to the needs of his sons, from whom he was growing increasingly distant. Gloria found herself drifting in a soulless marriage, with the father of her sons mostly absent.

She came to realise that her dream of replicating the warm and loving family in which she was raised and for which she yearned, had slowly faded and died. She asked Daniel for a divorce, to which he readily agreed. It was an amicable arrangement, but it left Gloria heartbroken. Her world was shattered, and she found herself adrift amid the debris of her marriage.

Feeling disconnected from the world in which he found himself, Max decided to return to college to complete his law degree. Yetta, sensing her son's distress, encouraged him. It was her contention that Max would blunt his pain by immersing himself in study, and her prediction proved correct. Max was a handsome, eligible bachelor and was readily welcomed into the social set of his peers. The thrumming of campus life included many social engagements and Max was soon caught up in a whirl of studies and activities as the fast pace of New York tightened its grip.

And yet ... Helena hovered on the periphery of his memory, and hugged the shadows of the night cast by a lemony New York moon. But her features blurred and dimmed as he became caught up in the rhythm of his fast-paced life.

The silver candlesticks belonging to Samuel's Russian mother, the candlesticks Yetta carried to America, were prominently displayed on the mantelpiece in the Harris home. It was only as Yetta lit her Sabbath candles, her hands hovering over the flame that flooded the room with light, that Max was able to recreate Helena's face as he took the seat vacated by Samuel at the head of the table.

Chapter 14

PARIS

1947

Edie's flamboyant style and untamed coal-black curls tied back with a purple bandana attracted Helena the day she arrived at Pompadour. Edie, a Hungarian refugee, was a talented designer who headed up Pompadour's design team. Helena was fascinated by Edie's ability to embroider intricate designs onto fabric, as she cut and twirled brightly-coloured ribbons to complete the hats before they were shipped off to boutiques along the Champs-Élysées.

The air in the factory was constantly filled with the whirr of sewing machines and the chatter of the workers. It was only the shrill siren signalling their lunch breaks that silenced the noise as the workers scattered to the cafeteria.

Sitting across from Edie on the cafeteria bench one lunchtime, Helena caught her eye and smiled shyly at her. The following day Edie joined Helena for lunch. She could sense the vulnerability of this quiet, serene girl with the luminous eyes; eyes that revealed the pain in the depths of her soul. She reached out to her and soon their lunches together became a daily ritual. As their trust in each other grew, they shared stories of their past. Edie confided to Helena that when she lived in Hungary and war broke out, it was the family maid, Nora, who saved her parents and herself and so she related Norah's story.

Nora considered herself fortunate. After leaving her home on the farm where she had been raised, to seek work in the city, she had found employment with a Jewish family. Dr Jozsef was an eminent surgeon and he and his wife, Lena, and their daughter, Edie, treated her well. Lena taught Nora to cook and mend, and Edie befriended her, although Edie was a few years younger than Nora. They shared confidences and exchanged movie magazines, leading to lively discussions about the latest movie stars. Whenever she returned to the farm to visit her own family, Nora was laden with food parcels and little gifts for her numerous siblings.

Zoe was Nora's oldest sibling. When Zoe's two-year-old son Janos fell gravely ill and it seemed he might die, Nora implored Dr Jozsef to help her nephew. The doctor admitted the child to the hospital in which he practised, and personally nursed Janos back to health. The grateful family felt a burden of debt to him.

When it became evident that the lives of the Jews in Hungary were in peril, Nora's family devised a plan to save the doctor and his family. Disguised as farm workers, Jozsef, Lena and Edie were taken into Nora's home on the farm. They ploughed the fields, harvested crops and milked cows, hidden among the other farm workers.

In this way, Dr Jozsef, Lena and Edie evaded the Nazis until the war ended and they were able to flee to the safety of the camps for displaced persons across the border in Austria.

Nora's family's debt to Dr Jozsef was repaid three times. Edie's family chose to remain in Vienna in the camps for displaced and stateless people. Edie, herself having witnessed the upheaval and destruction of so many comfortable middle-class lives, was determined to find a permanent home in Palestine. Joint helped her reach Paris after the Nazi occupation of the city had come to an end, and she hoped to obtain an entry visa to Palestine through her connections with Bricha.

Recounting her own story to Edie, Helena saw her life fragmented as through a broken mirror. Tears sprung to Edie's eyes as Helena spoke of the events of the last few years. She was filled with wonder at Helena's tenacity in overcoming inconceivable cruelty and deeply moved by her bravery and resourcefulness. Swallowing the knot of tears in her throat she took Helena's hand in her own.

"You are a beacon of courage, Helena. You need to acknowledge your strength and celebrate your survival. In your journey you have been severely tested, but you are no longer a victim. Now it is your time to fight back."

Edie's words bolstered Helena's hope and made her more determined to rebuild her broken life. She would take advantage of all the possibilities offered to her.

The humming of machines, the twirling of ribbons and the creation of hats formed the backdrop to the friendship that blossomed between Edie and Helena. The factory floor was fertile ground for whispered secrets. Helena had noticed a glow about Edie and a rosy blush to her cheeks whenever Pierre lingered at her workplace. An undercurrent of whispers, nudges and knowing glances vibrated throughout the factory.

"Tell me your secret," said Helena teasingly, as she and Edie shared their lunch hour.

A broad smile lit Edie's face. "Pierre and I are getting married this summer," she said, giggling behind her hand, her almond-shaped eyes shining.

"I rejoice at your good news." Helena hugged her friend. A serious expression replaced her playfulness, and she blinked as a thought struck her. "What about your intention to reach Palestine? Is this also Pierre's wish?"

Edie became thoughtful. A shadow passed across her face and her eyes were downcast. When she looked up at Helena, she replied confidently.

"Pierre and I have decided to remain in Paris for now. Europe and Palestine are still in turmoil. The future is unclear but we love each other and we will make decisions together as time unravels and settles the problem. Pierre is my anchor and has given me a sense of belonging." She smiled at her friend, her eyes sparkling: "But Helena," she exclaimed, "I have made a contact for you; I will pass it on to you within the next few days. It will be all you will need for you and Rachel to secure your passage to Palestine."

Helena's heart flickered with hope as she felt the excitement radiating from Edie.

"Meanwhile," said Edie, "we have a wedding to plan, and I will need your help to make it perfect."

"Oh Edie," said Helena as she threw her arms around her friend. "It will be the most perfect wedding, and you will be the most beautiful bride."

The days slipped by and Helena waited with anxious anticipation for any sign of the contact Edie had promised. But as the days become weeks her hope began to fade.

The lingering afternoon sun casts long shadows, turning the dust in the factory to gold. It was the end of another day at Pompadour and Helena was preparing to leave. Slipping the sling of her bag over her head, she heard Edie softly call her name. With a warning finger to her lips, Edie gestured to Helena to remain behind. Once they were alone, she pushed a folded note into Helena's hand.

"Give this to Jacques. Tell him to memorise the details and then destroy it," Edie whispered, as she too prepared to leave. "Be careful."

Rivulets of sweat pooled at the base of Helena's spine as she reached the Blums' apartment on the Rue des Rosiers, having run most of the way. Breathlessly she burst into Jacques' study. He was hunched over a radio, turning the dials and listening intently for any news over the crackling airwaves. Helena thrust the note at him, repeating Edie's instructions.

Jacques nodded as he studied the contents of the note. Exhaling through his mouth he placed his elbows on the table, dropping his head into his hands. Then he looked up triumphantly. "This is what I have been searching for, Lenie, and now I have the right contact. Please tell Amelie that I will be dining in my study tonight."

With a wave of his hand, he turned back to the radio and Helena was dismissed.

Comfortingly familiar sounds spilled in through the window as Helena tossed restlessly in her bed. A night owl hooted in the inky blackness and a light breeze ruffled the curtain at the open window. Somewhere in the distance a clock chimed the hour, the sound echoing in the still night air. The wind had picked up, billowing the curtain inwards. Helena imagined that the sound she heard was carried on the wind. She leaned over and closed the bedroom window but the sound persisted. It was then that she grasped that the sound was that of muffled voices and was drifting towards her from Jacques' study. Now fully alert, she sat bolt upright straining to catch an occasional word.

The sky was lightening as dawn crept in and the birds had begun their morning chorus when she padded on bare feet towards the study. A sliver of light shone under the door and Helena pushed it open. Jacques was still hunched over the spluttering, hissing shortwave radio from which the voices had come. She saw exhaustion etched into the creases of his face and noted his dishevelled appearance and bleary eyes. It seemed to her as though he has not slept all night.

Helena stood in the doorway, framed by the light. Jacques' eyes softened as he caught sight of her and gestured for her to enter.

She settled into a seat beside him and, turning to her, Jacques placed his elbow on the desk top and lowered his forehead into his palm. Then he looked up thoughtfully.

"Lenie, you and Rachel will be sailing within the next few months on board the *S.S. Providence* from Marseilles to Palestine. Papers, documents and visas are now being prepared that will assure you both of a safe passage."

Helena was engulfed in a tangle of emotions, and her eyes widened in disbelief at Jacques' words. With a catch in her throat, she asked, "How did this happen, Uncle?"

Jacques sighed deeply and rubbed his eyes with the heels of his hands. He sat quietly collecting his thoughts. In the silence, Helena could hear the sound of her own breath as she waited for him to speak. When he broke the silence, he spoke in hushed undertones, relaying to Helena the sequence of events that unfolded after she had delivered Edie's note to him.

The man code-named 'Colonel Henderson' was a high-ranking officer in Churchill's government and an undercover operative for Bricha. His identity was closely guarded, known only to a few senior Bricha agents. The antipathy towards the British for turning back shiploads of desperate survivors caused many countries to assist Bricha in smuggling survivors into Palestine. The risk to the survivors was that should they be caught, they would be sent to British internment camps in Cyprus.

Through Colonel Henderson, documents could be arranged for Jewish immigrants to reach Palestine, breaking the British embargo. It was this top-secret contact that Edie had passed on to Helena. Colonel Henderson's identity was encoded and connecting with him meant transmissions passing through multiple layers of cryptically-coded identities. Jacques, being well connected to the Underground, had already obtained many of these codes but the contact that Edie produced was the one at the top of the chain, the ultimate decision-maker who could break through the barrier and connect him finally to Colonel Henderson.

Throughout the night Jacques was passed along the chain of authority from one contact to the other until, at last, he reached Colonel Henderson. He had waited interminably for call-backs verifying his identity. When he was finally connected, arrangements were hurriedly finalised for travel documents for Helena and Rachel that would guarantee them a safe passage to Palestine. Then the line went dead and Jacques was left holding a humming receiver.

Helena listened intently, riveted by Jacques' story. When it dawned on her that her dream of Rachel and herself reaching Palestine was about to be fulfilled, she threw her arms around Jacques, knowing that no words could ever adequately convey her gratitude. Bleary-eyed, Jacques gently pushed her away.

"Lenie, I am going to sleep now, and I suggest that you do the same," he said wearily.

But Helena knew that sleep would be impossible. She was fully awake and tingling with excitement; she needed to share the news with Rachel. Gently she opened Rachel's bedroom door and found her asleep under the bedcovers, her nightcap having slipped over her eyes.

Helena stood at the bedside until Rachel sensed her presence. She sat up abruptly, rubbing the sleep from her eyes.

"*Schatzi*, why are you here? What is the matter?" she yawned.

"Move over, Rachel." Helena said climbing in beside her beneath the bedcovers. She curled against the warmth of Rachel's body and in breathless whispers she related the events of the past few hours.

Tears of joy wet Rachel's cheeks as she hugged Helena. The faces of her murdered family floated before her. "When we reach Palestine, I shall lay a headstone in the cemetery for each of my children, my husband and my parents. I do not know where their bodies lie, but by doing that it will give me closure and I will have a place to visit and to pray for their souls. Their memories must be preserved forever," she murmured, as though in prayer.

By the time the crimson dawn had turned to gold, Rachel's comforting warmth had soothed Helena and she succumbed at last to sleep.

Chapter 15

PARIS

1945-1947

A week before the much-anticipated wedding, the atmosphere at Pompadour was electric with excitement. At the machines, the hats had been surreptitiously pushed aside to make way for the creation of gowns to be worn to the wedding by the workers. Splendid creations in satin, lace and velvet emerged while seamstresses with pins clenched between their lips adjusted seams and pinned up hemlines.

Taking note of the frenzied activities, Pierre smiled indulgently and turned a blind eye as he too got caught up in the heightened atmosphere.

Amelie had arranged for her personal seamstress to fashion gowns for the women of her household. Her own Chantilly lace full-length gown complemented her creamy skin, willowy figure and shining dark hair. Rachel chose a vibrant green satin gown that highlighted her hazel eyes. Daring to be different, Helena was determined to wear a knee-length dress in black velvet with a white lace trim at the neckline and cuffs. It was a replica of one she'd seen in a fashion magazine. She twirled in front of the mirror, smiling happily at her reflection.

A buttery sun that blurred the morning into a haze heralded

the wedding day. The manicured lawn of Pierre's home behind the Eiffel Tower was the perfect setting for the ceremony. The air was heavy with the fragrant scent of roses and gardenias. Poppies and pansies trembled in the light breeze, nodding as if in greeting to the butterflies that perched on them, while a lucent blue sky provided the backdrop for the wedding scene. At the bottom of the garden four young men constructed a shimmering white fringed canopy under which Pierre would marry his beloved Edie.

Later in the day, guests began congregating and filling up the seats set out for them on the lawn. They waited in feverish anticipation for the arrival of the bride. They didn't have long to wait. On a carpet of white rose petals, as the weeping strains of a violin picked up the Wedding March, a radiant Edie appeared.

Ethereal in her gossamer white lace gown, a crown of gardenias adorning her dark curls, she drew gasps of admiration from the guests. Pierre, handsome in a top hat and tails, turned to greet his bride as she circled around him seven times, while handkerchiefs were discreetly dabbed at eyes.

The shattering of the glass after the vows were concluded was a reminder of the fragility of happiness and the vulnerability of relationships.

Rachel, Helena and the Blums threw themselves with gusto into the celebrations that followed. Pierre and Edie were raised up in ribbon-decorated chairs while the dancing guests encircled them. Tables groaned under the weight of platters filled with French delicacies and champagne flowed to a chorus of *L'Chaim – To Life!*

As the sun dipped over the horizon and the first stars

appeared, the guests became more adventurous. The American Allies had introduced chewing gum, Coca-Cola and the latest dance craze, the Jitterbug to France. The wedding party provided the perfect opportunity to try out the steps. Enthusiastically they bounced and hopped, jerking to the fast tempo before collapsing breathlessly in each other's arms as the music ended.

The light of a milky moon guided the wedding guests as they made their way home. A horse-drawn open carriage was brought up the driveway of Pierre's home, ready to carry the bridal couple away for the beginning of a new chapter of their lives. While being helped into the carriage, Edie turned back and her eyes met Helena's. She silently mouthed "Thank you" before throwing her bouquet of white roses into Helena's arms.

It had been a perfect wedding day, with Joy the guest whose presence was most felt.

Chapter 16

POLAND
1946-1947

It was morning in Nadia's garden, the dew still fresh on the grass and the vegetables were a riot of colour. Sun-ripened tomatoes, sumptuous green lettuces and bright orange pumpkins grew in profusion. Nestled among the foliage under the overhanging branch of a Birch tree Nadia had laid out a blanket to sit on. Sofia lay next to her, her head cradled in Nadia's lap. A breeze rustled through the branches of the birch tree causing the catkins to float down to the dewy grass. Nadia stroked Sofia's hair while softly crooning to her. Sofia's frail body had wasted to that of a child, her skin so pale that it appeared translucent against the white cotton nightgown that fitted loosely on her slight frame.

Dr Anton Fischer, who lived in the cottage next to Nadia's, had been caring for Sofia since she arrived in Poland a year ago. However, since the Russians took control of Poland, medicines had been in short supply and much-needed penicillin was unobtainable. Nadia initially attempted to flee with Sofia to Vienna in the hope of finding medication and more qualified doctors to help her recover in the hospitals there. They had joined a group trying to escape Poland through the forests at night. But a weakened Sofia held the group back and Nadia and

Sofia were forced to return to the cottage while the rest of the group managed to cross the border into Vienna.

"Tell me the moonbeam story," murmured Sofia, her voice so faint that Nadia had to lower her head to hear her.

"Not again!" Nadia smiled, amused that Sofia never tired of hearing the childhood story that she'd repeated so often to the sisters, Anna and Sofia Abron, in the time she cared for them before the war. She settled Sofia's head more comfortably in her lap, covered her with a light woollen shawl, and began to tell the story once more.

"All the little moonbeams lived peacefully on Mother Moon, happily playing catch-the-moonbeam among the stars. Some nights they would float down to earth and into the bedrooms of the sleeping children, but soon they became discontented. The children's lives seemed so much more exciting than their own uneventful existence. So, they asked Mother Moon to let them live on Mother Earth. She agreed, but she warned them: 'If you decide to come back home you will never be allowed to visit Mother Earth again.' And so the little moonbeams floated down to Mother Earth and into the homes of the earthling children.

"But their joy was short-lived. In the earthling homes they heard angry voices, and laughter was often mingled with tears. They encountered daily struggles and discovered that on Mother Earth there were wars, hunger and not much peace, unlike their lives on Mother Moon. So, they decided that life was, after all, better on Mother Moon and they glided back home to her. Mother Moon was overjoyed to have her moonbeams back and she glowed with pride so brightly that every night the earthlings gazed in awe at the brilliance of the golden moon that hung suspended in the star-speckled sky."

Sofia's delicate eyelids closed as Nadia ended the story, her lips curled in a contented smile. Nadia scooped her up and carried her inside to await the doctor's daily visit.

Dr Anton Fischer was a tall, lumbering figure. Tufts of hair threaded with white grew at angles around his otherwise bald head. The gold-rimmed glasses perched at the end of his nose did little to hide the sorrow he felt for his young patient. Once he examined Sofia, Nadia walked with him to the door leading outside. Wiping the mist from his glasses with his handkerchief, he turned to her.

"I have done all I can for Sofia, and so have you," he said gravely. "Stay at her side and call me when you need me."

All day Nadia sat at Sofia's bedside listening to her laboured breathing. As the afternoon shadows lengthened into dusk, she lay down beside Sofia, holding her hand, while humming childhood lullabies and cradle songs to her. It was the darkest hour of night, just before dawn, when Sofia gave one last shuddering breath. Nadia lit a candle at the foot of the bed and pulled a woollen shawl over her own head and shoulders.

Before calling for Dr Fischer, she opened the bedroom window and watched the moonbeams float away while a pendulous moon cast a halo in the cloudless sky.

Chapter 17

PARIS
1947

The incessant ringing of the telephone in the Blums' apartment pierced the still night, tearing the occupants from their sleep. Jacques, barefoot and not yet fully awake, was the first to reach it, followed by the women, who were still rubbing the sleep from their eyes. With a sense of foreboding, Jacques lifted the receiver to his ear.

He covered the receiver with one hand and turned to the women. "This is a call from Poland ... 'Allo." He spoke into the receiver again. "'Allo. Who is this? Nadia? Yes, yes, I can hear you." He listened intently, straining to hear down the buzzing phone line.

Then Jacques drew in his breath and emitted a deep, drawn-out sigh. The colour drained from his face. "I will put Helena on the line." He handed the receiver to Helena who stood rigidly beside him, her eyes burning questioningly into his.

Nadia repeated the sombre news of Sofia's passing. Helena listened in shocked disbelief. Then, wracked by heaving, shuddering sobs, she crumpled, inconsolable to the ground. Rachel and Jacques stood by helplessly trying to comfort her. Amelie busied herself preparing warm milk for what was going to be a long and sleepless night.

As the first light of a new dawn filtered through the window, Helena, spent with raw emotion, finally fell asleep tucked against the warm curve of Rachel's body. Rachel's presence was consoling and soothed Helena. Her solidness was a source of strength to her.

"We will continue to light our Sabbath candles for you, little Sofia," Rachel whispered into the darkness. "We will never forget you. Your bravery will be a shining beacon for Helena and me and for future generations. I shall lay a stone for you too when we reach Palestine".

Then sleep washed over her, silencing her troubled thoughts.

A steel-grey late afternoon light ushered in the evening as the two lone figures of Rachel and Helena, with heads bowed, stood before the flickering flames of the memorial candles. The light cast their silhouettes against the wall. A pall of gloom clung to the air, made denser by the stillness of the figures. A group of men were being led by the elderly, stooped rabbi whose long, grey beard reached almost to his waist. Soulfully, they intoned the Kaddish prayer for Sofia, a prayer to elevate the soul of the deceased to a higher realm.

The death of Sofia left Helena with a devastating sense of loss. She had nurtured a fragile thread of hope that she and Sofia would rebuild their lives in Palestine, sharing memories of their childhood before the war.

Now these memories would be Helena's alone and the responsibility of preserving their legacies would rest solely with her. Her promise of meeting Sofia in Palestine would never be fulfilled.

It was the last of the seven nights of prayers. Amelie would remove the covers from the mirrors to signify the end of the week of mourning. The ancient rituals had been a source of comfort to Helena and had provided all of them with a sense of connection.

At the conclusion of the prayers, the rabbi stood before Helena and held his hands above her head as he blessed her for a long and good life. Helena lifted her tear-stained face to meet his gaze. "Rabbi," she said, her voice heavy with grief. "You have blessed me for a long life, but how will I bear my loss? And why have I survived when Sofia and so many others have not?"

Hearing the heartbreak in her voice, the rabbi closed his eyes contemplatively for a few moments. Then he spoke slowly, his speech stilted with a heavy Yiddish accent.

"Helena, you were destined to survive to be the messenger for all future generations so that the depravity perpetrated on an innocent people may never happen again, and that there should be tolerance of all religions. It was not your choice to make as to who would survive and who would not.

"You have shown such courage. Go to Palestine, fulfil your dream and nurture forever the memory of Sofia and your loved ones. But never lose faith in the good of humanity and never forget that hate is destructive and that love is the most powerful force of all."

The rabbi's words struck a deep chord and stirred up a memory. It dawned on Helena that even in her darkest moments there had always been a glimmer of light. Ironically, it was the reminiscence of a Nazi officer in the camp that caused the rabbi's words to resonate with her.

It had been a gloomy day with heavy grey clouds scudding across a darkening sky. Helena, her shoulders hunched over the cart she pushed across the camp, felt her muscles contort with pain. Hunger consumed her. It was many hours since she had been given a portion of hard bread. A bowl of watery soup was all she had to look forward to at the end of the day. How she longed for Cook Berta's wholesome meals. The thought of borscht and dumplings made her stomach growl with hunger.

The cloying stench of death, carried on the thick black smoke emanating from the crematoria, lay heavy in the air. The ever-present harsh shouts of the guards and the ominous rifle shots that surrounded her were a reminder of the constant threat to the security of her life. The Nazi guards could administer death at any moment as a punishment for an imagined offence.

A soldier, rifle in hand, stepped across Helena's path and ordered her to accompany him to the guardroom in the watchtower. A shudder of fear gripped her, constricting her breath, and she recoiled at his threatening demeanour. Nausea rose in her throat. The menacing expression in the officer's eyes reinforced her conviction that his intentions were evil.

It felt as though time slowed down as she followed him into the guardroom.

"Go to the officers' mess and bring my dinner back to me," he barked at her.

Stricken with terror, barely able to walk, Helena carried out his instruction, returning with a layered tray containing a three-course meal of soup, meat and vegetables and an apple pie dessert. Helena handed the tray to him then attempted to leave quickly through the open door. But he closed and locked the door behind her. Waves of panic threatened to overwhelm her. And then, incredulously, she watched his features soften and he lowered his voice, ordering her to sit down at the table.

"This meal is for you. Eat it quickly and go back to your barrack." He glanced nervously around the room.

Unhesitatingly, Helena devoured the meal before her. "Why have you done this for me?" she asked him.

A shadow of a smile crossed his face. "Go now," is all that he would say.

In his one unguarded moment, Helena detected a divine spark of humanity in the German soldier. Her guardian angel, firmly fixed on her shoulder, smiled happily that day.

Once the rabbi had blessed Helena and the prayers were concluded, he and the rest of the men, all warmly dressed against the cold, prepared to leave. A rush of frosty air greeted them as they filed out of the apartment. Amelie and Rachel bustled about the kitchen preparing the evening meal and Jacques wrapped an arm around Helena, steering her towards his study.

The familiarity of the room and the warmth emanating from the smouldering embers in the hearth behind the copper fender comforted Helena as she sank into the comfortable armchair beside Jacques. He settled back in his chair and folded his arms across his stomach.

"Lenie, they have arrived." A smile lit up his face.

Wide-eyed, Helena looked back questioningly at him.

"Your tickets, *ma chérie*," he exclaimed. "I have received your tickets and all the valid documents from Colonel Henderson in London. You and Rachel will be travelling by train to Marseille within the next few weeks. The *S.S. Providence* on which you will travel to Palestine will dock in Marseille after you arrive there."

Despite her grief, Helena's spirits lifted at his words.

Hesitatingly, he added, "Amelie and I shall miss you." His voice cracked with emotion.

"Rachel and I shall miss you too. You and Amelie have been our refuge, and because of you we could continue to dream." She lifted Jacques' hands tenderly in her own and laid her cheek against them, her tears spilling between his fingers.

Jacques' heart swelled with love for the daughter of his dead sister, and he was aware of the void that the departure of Rachel and Helena would leave in his and Amelie's lives.

Chapter 18

POLAND

1946

There is an eerie stillness in Nadia's cottage. She is seated in the chair from which she had watched over Sofia lying in bed for so many months. She rocks gently, clasping and unclasping her hands, her features drawn in grief. The only sound is that of the wind howling through the cracks.

Sofia was buried that morning. It was a simple service attended by ten Jewish men from the community as well as Dr Fischer and his family, Nadia, and a sprinkling of her friends. The young rabbi who conducted the service was deeply saddened at having to bury such a young girl, another victim of the Holocaust. He scooped up the first clod of earth with a spade and watched it fall with an echoing thud on Sofia's simple coffin. Expressing his deep sorrow, he turned the spade inwards and dug it back in the soil. For a few brief moments he stood pensively at the graveside, rocking back and forth in prayer.

All day, storm clouds have been gathering ominously. As night draws in, shrouding the cottage in darkness, the storm abandons itself. The heaving black clouds burst, releasing their burdon and drenching the parched earth below. The birch tree sways and bends in the ferocious wind and brushes up against the window. Swollen raindrops, like tears, roll down the windowpane.

"The universe grieves for Sofia," sighs Nadia.

The whistle of the kettle breaks the heavy silence. In the tiny kitchen she prepares a supper of buttered bread and tea, then carries it back to her seat and places it on the table beside her. But the bread remains uneaten and a milky layer on the tea congeals as Nadia's eyes drift closed.

Banging on her front door breaks into her dreamless sleep and she freezes, straining to distinguish the noise from that of the storm. The banging becomes more urgent, combined with a furious rattling of the door handle. She opens the door a crack and peers out into the stormy night.

Tomasz Nowak stands on the doorstep, soaked from the torrential rain, his wet hair plastered to his head. Nadia recognises him as the leader of an activist group that has been holding nightly meetings for many months to plan an escape route through the forest. They aimed to reach the border of Austria and the safety of the refugee camps.

Nadia's eyes widen in surprise.

"What are you doing here at this late hour? Come on inside and out of the storm." She has to raise her voice to be heard above the rush of the wind. She ushers him inside, pushes the door closed, and wraps a large towel around him before she refills the kettle to make fresh tea.

Wrapped in the towel, Tomasz sits on the bed facing her. He cradles the cup of steaming tea between his palms, leaning his elbows on his knees.

"Nadia, this is a sad time for you, for all of us, as we mourn the loss of Sofia. But I have come to tell you that we are leaving tomorrow night. You must come with us; this may be the only opportunity we have. The group is meeting in the town square tomorrow night, beneath the clock, as it strikes nine. Bring only essential items with you."

He searches her face eagerly, gauging her response.

Nadia turns around briefly, her eyes sweeping across the familiar cottage, and as her gaze comes to rest on Sofia's empty bed, she makes her decision. "I will be there," she answers firmly.

"Dress warmly, Nadia." Tomasz rises and rubs the towel over his wet hair before handing it back to her. "Thank you for the tea," he adds over his shoulder as he heads out of the cottage and back into the storm.

There is no need for sleep once the door closes behind Tomasz. In a cruel twist of fate, she will be leaving Poland at last – but without Sofia. She feels calm as she moves about the cottage, filling her rucksack. Sofia's nightdress, freshly washed, is folded among her few belongings. Nadia lifts it and presses the side of her face against it, breathing in Sofia's fragrance that still lingers on it. She brushes a tear away. She remembers that Tomasz said to bring only essential items with her. Impulsively, she thrusts that thought aside and places the nightdress in her rucksack.

"I will always keep you close, little Sofia," she whispers as she firmly closes the bag.

It is then that she notices the white envelope that has been lying beneath the nightdress. Sofia had addressed it to Helena in Paris and had asked Nadia to post it for her, but now it is too late. *I will give it to the doctor to slip into a letter box when I hand him the keys to the cottage,* she thinks.

The storm has run its course during the night and by morning branches torn from trees and uprooted saplings are strewn around the cottage. Nadia leaves the keys to her cottage, and the letter addressed to Helena, with Dr Fischer.

That evening, she joins the group that congregates underneath the clock. The light of the moon breaks through the clouds, guiding them on their way. Stealthily, they move through the forest, staying close to each other. There are children in the group and the men carry the littlest ones. Tomasz places branches and planks across the rivers and streams to enable them to cross.

They encounter a farmer, who allows them to spend the night on the hay in his barn. The next morning, they collect freshly-laid eggs from the henhouse and milk still warm from the cow. The farmer's wife prepares a satisfying breakfast for the group. They thank the couple for their kindness before they continue on their way through the dense forest.

Many days have passed since Tomasz and his group left Poland. Szymon Nowak, Tomasz's uncle, stands beneath the clock at the designated time. A passer-by briefly brushes against him, slipping a note into his hand before rushing off. Szymon unfolds the note and his face is wreathed in smiles as he reads it and punches the air in triumph. The group has arrived in Vienna and are securely housed in a refugee camp.

The mission is a success.

Chapter 19

NEW YORK
1945-1947

While Rachel and Helena had been settling into the Blums' household, across the ocean Max Harris was adjusting to the life of a New York law student. Memories of the evil and destruction that he had witnessed in Berlin after the war still cast an ominous shadow. In an attempt to bury the demons that haunted him, he surrounded himself with young men and women who, like him, worked hard and played even harder, intoxicated with life in post-war America. New York was a magical city with infinite possibilities.

That night, the Harris apartment on 5th Avenue was a hive of activity. A bevy of maids in freshly-starched white aprons, with dainty caps perched on their heads, were armed with dusters and mops. They collided with each other in their eagerness to spring-clean the apartment to perfection for the celebration which was to take place there that evening. Preparations were being finalised for Max's engagement to Jenny Singer. Yetta, determined to make this party the social event of the year, held court in the kitchen, conferring with the caterers as they ferried platters of canapés and cocktails across the highly-polished parquet floor.

Jenny was the daughter of Yetta's closest friend and bridge partner, Maeve Singer. Maeve's husband, Nate, was a successful optician in New York. The families met soon after arriving in America from Russia and quickly developed a close friendship. Yetta had felt that she was drifting on a cloud of happiness since Max announced this fine match.

A well-thumbed family album was among Yetta's treasured possessions. Black and white photographs taken on a Brownie camera filled the first pages; photographs of the radiant bridal couple, Yetta and Samuel, smiling into the camera, followed by those of Gloria and Max as babies. Further on in the album the photographs turned to colour, portraying the children growing up as Samuel and Yetta grew older. Prominently displayed near the back of the album was a photograph of a blonde, ponytailed Jenny Singer blowing out four candles on a birthday cake while a smiling, gap-toothed, six-year-old Max stood beside her. Max, Gloria and Jenny had been inseparable playmates, but as childhood turned to adolescence, their paths had drifted apart. A rather skinny, slightly buck-toothed Jenny was sent to school in Los Angeles while Max and Gloria's world expanded beyond their childhood experiences as they too came to stand on the threshold of adulthood.

Max was in his final year of law school when, during a lecture, his attention was drawn to a lithe, blonde woman near the front of the lecture hall. Her hand was always the first to shoot up in answer to the lecturer's questions. Max moved towards the front of the hall to get a better view of her. There was something strangely familiar about her and he blinked in disbelief as the thought came to him that this could be his childhood friend,

Jenny Singer. Still uncertain, he waited outside the hall after the lecture had ended. He was leaning against the pillar, hands deep in his pockets, when she appeared, confirming his suspicion. He drank her in with his eyes, noting the soft, blonde bob that brushed her shoulders and the pale blue sweater and pleated skirt that emphasised her curves. Hesitatingly he called to her.

She turned towards him and her blue eyes widened.

"Max?" Her voice quavered. Max strode towards her and stretched his arms wide open, folding her inside, breathing in her perfume.

Their joy at being reunited was mutual. Over numerous cups of coffee and many canteen sandwiches in the weeks that followed, they shared the events of the years they had spent apart. Max was struck by her beauty and intelligence and, looking into his gentle brown eyes, Jenny felt she had met her destiny. Encouraged by both families, Max and Jenny became inseparable. Jenny was part of the social set and their courtship was a whirl of cocktail parties and charity balls as their photographs appeared in the glossy society pages of newspapers and magazines.

In recounting the events of the intervening years, Max omitted much of the time he had spent in Berlin. He told her nothing about Helena. Time had softened the sharpness of the memory of the girl he thought he would never see again. But in the deep of night, when sleep was elusive, Helena's image would appear before him, tugging at his heart.

Putting aside all thoughts of Helena, Max felt as though his life had been mapped out to perfection. After all, Jenny Singer was the perfect fit for a future young attorney. She was sophisticated, smart and an accomplished hostess.

Blissfully unaware of the forces of nature and the vulnerability of man's proposals, a wedding was planned for the following summer.

Chapter 20

PARIS

1947

The days leading up to Rachel and Helena's departure were filled with sad goodbyes. At Pompadour the factory workers lined up to bid farewell to the soulful young woman they had come to love, each bearing messages of encouragement and small gifts. Helena hugged each one, thanking them for their friendship that supported her through the difficult days of settling in Paris after being liberated from the camps.

The evening before Rachel and Helena were due to leave Paris for their journey to Marseille, Pierre and Edie hosted a farewell party for them at their luxurious home. Edie had settled into married life with Pierre and that night she glowed with happiness in her ruby-red satin gown with strings of pearls looped around her neck and her dark hair newly styled into a fashionable bob.

It is the hour before the guests are due to arrive and Edie and Pierre are alone in their dressing room. Edie sits before her dressing table, studying her reflection in the large ornate mirror. She is putting the finishing touches to her hair and pouts as she carefully applies her lipstick.

Pierre, already dressed in an immaculate evening suit, is sprawled in an armchair behind her. His legs are casually crossed, his chin rests on his clenched fist. He appears pensive. He gazes at Edie brushing her hair and then rises and stands behind her. He rests his hands on her shoulders and bends to meet her eyes in the reflection of the mirror.

"You are so beautiful," he murmurs, "I am a fortunate man."

"I know that look on your face Pierre, what is it that troubles you?" replies Edie, narrowing her eyes.

Pierre walks towards the large picture window, overlooking the rolling lawns.

"It's Helena" he sighs, I am losing the best designer Pompadour has ever had. She has been an asset to the company and will be missed."

Edie walks across the room to where Pierre stands and threads her arms around his neck.

"And I am losing the closest friend I have ever had. But I am sure that this is not goodbye and that we will meet up again with Rachel and Helena in Palestine. They will always be a part of our lives."

Then, hand in hand, they descend the winding marble staircase to greet their guests.

The caterers were emptying the last platters as the guests, their good wishes trailing behind them, were leaving. Edie stood across the room, her eyes searching for Helena. She drew in her bottom lip and a look of pleasure crossed her face when she noticed how Helena had morphed into a beauty. The tangled blonde curls framing her delicate features emphasised her large blue eyes. Her slender frame, once so emaciated, had filled out pleasantly, enhanced by the softly-draped buttercup-yellow gown she wore. Rachel too, under Amelie's watchful eye, had transformed into a chic French madame and looked every bit the part in a knee-length gold embossed silk shift.

Edie crossed the marble floor to where Rachel and Helena were seeing off the last of the guests. She wrapped an arm around the shoulders of each of the women. "Go well, my dearest friends," she said, her voice trembling. "You have shown me that even in life's darkest hours there is beauty and grace to be found. I know we shall meet again in Palestine." She walked with them towards Pierre's car, which was waiting to drive them back to the Blums' apartment.

It had rained during the night and a watery winter sun was breaking through heavy grey clouds as day broke. Helena and Rachel, well prepared for their journey, waited patiently with their belongings at the entrance of the Blums' apartment. Amelie and Jacques would accompany them to the train station.

They piled into Jacques' new Renault convertible. Jacques had retracted the rooftop and the biting wind was exhilarating, rushing through their hair and stinging their cheeks to a rosy hue. They chatted brightly to each other, avoiding speaking of their deepest feelings, but their faces betrayed their emotions.

The circumstances that brought them together had bonded them more closely than most families. The women's departure would leave an emptiness in Jacques and Amelie's lives, and their absence would be felt in the quiet of the apartment. Rachel and Helena were leaving behind the sanctuary of the Blums' home and their cocooning warmth for an unpredictable future in an unknown land. All four felt an aching sense of sorrow as Rachel and Helena left the apartment for the last time.

At the train station they were swallowed up by the surging crowd. Steel trolleys filled with luggage rattled along the platform while instructions issued over loudhailers added to the tumult. The little group stood huddled together, delaying the moment of departure.

It crossed Jacques' mind that this was the same platform to which he had come to collect Rachel and Helena on their arrival from Berlin. A vision floated before him of the two women then, clutching their meagre belongings and looking uncertainly around them. He marvelled at the change in their demeanour brought about by the intervening years. There was a lightness about them now and a new-found confidence in the set of their shoulders.

The train steamed into the station, spewing thick grey smoke behind it, metal wheels screeching against metal rails as it slowly ground to a halt. Rachel embraced Amelie one last time.

"Thank you for opening the world to me. Your kindness has touched me deeply," she said, her eyes moist.

The four clung to each other until the uniformed and heavily-moustached conductor blew his whistle, urging Rachel and Helena to board the train. Before they were ushered aboard, Jacques drew Helena and Rachel close and recited the prayer for the safety of travellers. It was the same prayer that his father, Mendel, had blessed him with when he left Poland.

As the train shunted out of the station the women hung out of the window, waving at the receding figures of Jacques and Amelie until the train rounded a curve and they could be seen no more.

Chapter 21

MARSEILLE

Helena strode along the seafront. Seagulls wheeled about, darting at their prey in the cobalt-blue sea. A breeze whipped sharply at her, leaving its salty residue on her skin, and she lifted her chin to the sun to warm her face.

On their arrival in Marseille, Rachel and Helena were embraced by the community of refugees and volunteers. Poignant moments were shared when inmates last seen in the camps reappeared and heart-wrenching stories were exchanged. The sadness in their eyes reflected the dark places from where they had come. All had lost family members – all grieved. Why did the world remain pitilessly silent despite being aware of the evil being perpetrated by the Nazis in Europe? That was the question most asked. When no answers could be found, heads turned away as men and women sought solace in each other and in the work allotted to them.

The coast of Marseille was strewn with a colony of houses that accommodated the newly-arrived immigrants, the survivors of the death camps of Europe now bound for Palestine. Many were displaced people without any identification or possessions. They were unable to return to their homes in Eastern Europe, as Russia controlled the Eastern Bloc. Nor were they able to pass the British embargo; shiploads of refugees bearing false papers and destined for Palestine had been turned back by the British. Many were sent to camps in Cyprus to await eventually being sent on to Palestine.

Only after independence and the declaration of the State of Israel would this come to pass. Then only would they be welcomed as proud citizens of their own homeland. Rachel carried their documents in a pouch secured to her clothing, knowing that thanks to 'Colonel Henderson' in London, their papers were valid and stamped with entry visas.

For now, the immigrants waited patiently for vessels that would carry them to their destination. To fill the waiting hours, they packed the docked ships with sufficient provisions to sustain the passengers for their sea journey.

Filip was one of the immigrants at the camp. He was extremely tall and gaunt. His angular features had retained their haunted look since his arrival at Marseille from Bergen-Belsen. His eyes, sunken deep into their sockets, his protruding nose and his close-cropped hair, gave him a ghoulish appearance.

Helena and Rachel were helping to prepare the Exodus for its sea journey to Palestine when Filip approached Helena. He smiled at her, displaying broken, discoloured teeth.

"It is so good to meet you here and to know that you have survived," he said. "Do you remember me?"

He cocked his head to the side, and the movement caused the memory of a scene in Bergen-Belsen to flash clearly before her.

"Y-you gave me my first mouthful of food," she exclaimed, her eyes widening.

Filip nodded in acknowledgement. "We were abandoned by the Nazis at the end of the war and left without food and water. Only snow sustained us. I was among a few of the surviving men who had the strength to open tins of food left behind by the Nazis. You were barely conscious when I placed a spoonful of sauerkraut on your tongue."

Helena took his bony hands in both of hers. "I shall forever remember the glorious taste of that mouthful of sauerkraut, as well as your kindness," she said, as the recalled memory became crystal clear. "But when did you arrive in Marseille?"

"I left Germany a few months ago and have been here ever since. Tonight, I am sailing aboard this ship, together with the group I came with, to Palestine. I hope that we shall meet again." He smiled shyly.

"I do, too," Helena nodded eagerly.

Then they turned and went their separate ways. All the crew and passengers aboard the ill-fated Exodus, never did get to disembark in Palestine.

The sonorous sound of the waves crashing against the rocks and the warmth of the sun on her limbs caused Helena's thoughts to drift back to her brief meeting with Filip. She recalled the events that had brought her to this moment and decisions she had made which now shaped her life.

She was filled with sorrow whenever she remembered Sofia and the promise they made to each other to meet in

Palestine. That promise would never be kept, but Sofia's memory strengthened Helena's desire to rebuild her broken world and to forge a path towards a new life in a new land. She would perpetuate the heritage of those who would never have the opportunity to reach the safety of a land of their own. The thought gave her courage to face an uncertain future.

Max's features had blurred with time but still, when she lit her Sabbath candles, she recalled the boy with the gentle eyes who lifted her from the abyss of overwhelming despair and enabled her to embrace life once again.

Her reverie was broken by the strident hooting of a ship in the distance. Tenting her eyes with her hands, she peered out to sea and spotted a ship on the horizon which grew steadily larger as it steamed towards the harbour. Then it appeared in full view, its name emblazoned on the side of the hull. The *S.S. Providence* had arrived.

Turning away from the seafront Helena rushed from the beach towards Rachel, calling out to her that the ship had arrived. She part-ran, part-stumbled her arms flailing excitedly. Sea spray stung her cheeks while her calls to Rachel mingled with the cawing of the gulls and the roar of the waves.

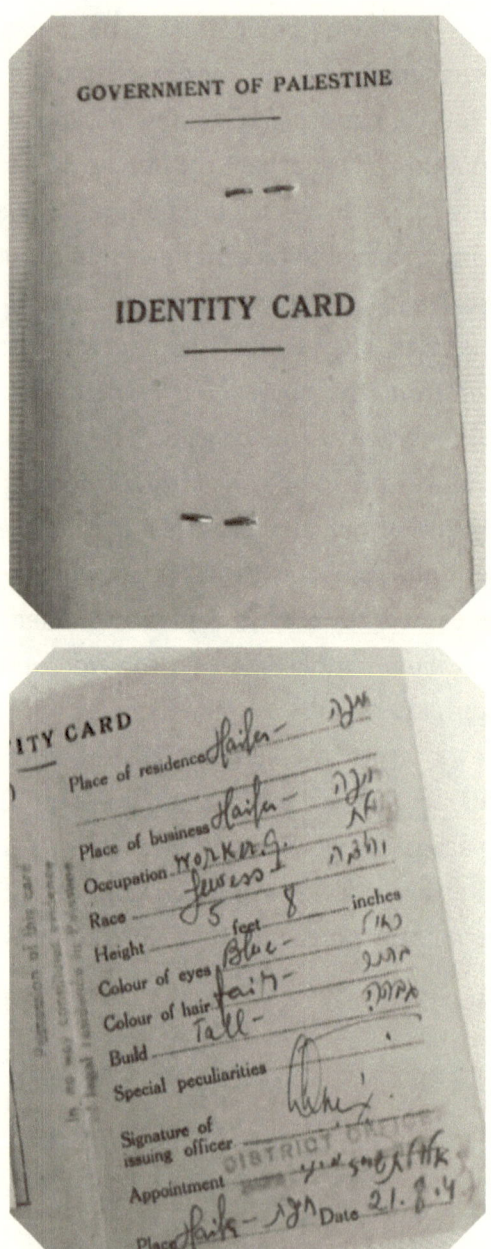

'Valid' documents allowing entry into Palestine.

PART TWO

PALESTINE - ISRAEL

Chapter 22

AUTUMN 1947

An impossibly-blue sky reflecting an indigo sea was the backdrop of the S.S. Providence as it sailed into Haifa. Closer to shore, the turquoise hues of the sea sparkled beneath a blisteringly hot sun that bleached the sandy shore to an iridescent white.

Boats filled with well-wishers, some offering refreshments, churned up the water as they sailed alongside the Providence. As the ship entered the harbour groups of onlookers eagerly scanned the passengers for familiar faces, shielding their eyes against the blinding light.

Rachel and Helena stood on the sun-drenched deck as the harbour came into view. The painful tears they had shed over the years since their internment were replaced with tears of joy. They stretched out their arms to the waiting crowd. Groups of passengers standing at the railings on the deck of the ship spontaneously broke into joyous song. The passengers were welcomed ashore by a jubilant crowd of settlers, eager to welcome the survivors into their community. These survivors were a handful who had miraculously survived the near annihilation of a nation, and they were warmly received. Once ashore, Rachel and Helena knelt to touch the soil.

"*Schatzi ...*" said Rachel, who was crouching on the ground on which she spreads her open palms. "Our journey has brought us here to fulfil the promise made to the souls of our loved ones, and we bring these souls here with us. May the lives of these brave people be avenged".

"Now let us test Colonel Henderson's documents."

Rachel retrieved the treasured visas from the pouch firmly secured around her waist, and she and Helena again successfully passed through British customs. Relieved, they boarded the bus that would transport them to a kibbutz close to Haifa.

On the kibbutz, they met acquaintances from their hometowns and family friends among the residents who arrived in Palestine before the war as volunteers. They met up with immigrants from across Europe who, like themselves, carried the scars of their desperate struggle for survival but were eager to begin a new life in the safety of their own homeland.

Helena was elated to meet the settlers who had befriended her grandparents. They were able to give her a personal account of Sheina and Mendel from the time of their arrival in Palestine, also mentioning the couple's sorrow at having lost all communication with their family in Poland. The only word they received, and that rarely, was from their son, Jacob, in Paris. His letters informed them of the extent of the devastation left by the Nazis as they barrelled their way through Europe. The news brought them no comfort, but they continued to hope that they would be reunited with their loved ones.

Tali Simons was a small-boned woman with sharp features and fluttery gestures, which gave her a birdlike appearance.

Her gnarled hands and weathered cheeks reflected the harsh conditions that the immigrants had endured. She wore her long, grey hair rolled back into a bun in the nape of her neck and had a voluminous apron with deep pockets tied around her waist. Her friendly manner and ready smile made her a popular member of the kibbutz.

When Tali met Helena she embraced her.

"I knew your grandparents. We left Europe on the same ship before the war. They were fine people; a devoted couple who were respected by all the immigrants," she told an enraptured Helena.

"We were living in a small town on the hills of Jerusalem. I was much younger than Sheina, yet we became close companions. I took care of her when Mendel passed away, although she didn't live much longer. She simply couldn't survive without him. But child ..." Tali placed her hands on Helena's shoulders, and looking deep into her eyes she said: "I have a gift for you. Before Sheina died she gave me her prayerbook. Keep it safe," she said, "and give it to my granddaughters, should any of them survive. My last wish is that they should have it."

"I have kept it, always hoping for this moment, and now that I have found you, on behalf of Sheina I hand it to you." Tali dug into the deep pocket of her apron and withdrew Sheina's prayerbook.

Overcome with emotion, Helena clasped it with both her hands, holding it close to her chest. The knot in her throat rendered her unable to speak. The pages of the prayerbook had yellowed with age and use; for Helena it was a rare and precious gift.

Being absorbed into the community gave Rachel and Helena a sense of connection and they soon adjusted to the rhythm of life on the kibbutz.

They were woken by the crowing of roosters signalling the break of dawn. All day they toiled alongside the deeply-tanned, hard-working inhabitants, mixing easily with their fellow workers as they milked cows and hoed crops. They learned ways of dealing with the heat, while their muscles grew strong and their skins turned to gold. The children's voices raised in song followed them throughout the day.

It was at twilight, when all the workers gathered around the campfire for the evening meal, everyone joining in with the singing of the children, that Rachel and Helena were filled with a contentment they thought they had forgotten. As night closed in, they made their way towards their cabin, the starlit sky providing the only light.

It was on such a night that a child stepped across their path. Starlight illuminated the sandy hair that swept across the boy's forehead in a heavy fringe and the fine dusting of pale freckles across his nose. He stood poised as though he had been waiting for them. When the women approached him, he turned his clear grey eyes up to Helena.

"Helena, do you know who I am?" he asked, a pleading note creeping into his voice. Helena imagined that she had seen the boy among the children singing around the campfire but, puzzled, she shook her head. Then she took a step closer to the boy and with her index finger beneath his chin she tilted his face close to hers.

"Who are you?" she asked, bewildered.

He stretched up his arms to her. "I am Adam. You protected and cared for me when we were both in Auschwitz." he answered, struggling to gulp down a sob.

For a moment Helena was rooted in shock. Then, tentatively, she reached out, pushing his hair back from his forehead and studied his features. She screwed up her eyes, trying to reconcile the face of the child she remembered in Auschwitz with that of the boy on the cusp of adulthood standing before her and she felt a sense of connection.

"Adam," she whispered, disbelief coursing through her veins. She clasped him in her arms so tightly it was as though he might disappear if she were to let him go. "You have survived." Her throat was tight with raw emotion. "You were so young when we were separated that I didn't think it would be possible for you to survive."

Adam, with all his defences down, wound his arms around her neck. "You were all I had when I was separated from my family, and I owe my life to you."

Rachel had been standing to one side, mesmerised by the scene being played out. She turned her head rapidly from Helena to Adam, absorbing their story, then threw her arms up in the air.

"This is another miracle," she exclaimed. She wrapped an arm around Helena and Adam and steered them to the warmth of the cabin.

Once inside, Rachel scuttled about. Swiftly she produced a jug of creamy milk and buttered wedges of newly-baked bread, still moist and warm, which they ate with Adam sitting between the women on one of the wooden cots. Helena and Rachel exchanged surreptitious glances when they observed Adam grab at the food and quickly stuff it into his mouth. Sadly, it would take time for the boy to come to accept that food was plentiful and that he would never again have to suffer the pain of hunger he experienced in the camp. With the turning years, he would eventually become aware that he no longer needed to grab at, or even steal, food ever again.

Deep into the night, Adam and Helena recalled their shared experiences.

Helena had found the child wandering about the camp. Having recently arrived in Auschwitz, he was bewildered, starving and filthy. At the sight of the trembling little boy something inside Helena broke. She sensed her need for human contact mirrored in him. When she approached him, he backed away and folded his arms defensively across his body. Then she knelt and held out her arms to him and hesitantly, he allowed her to draw him into her embrace. Helena cradled the bony little body against hers until the fluttering of his heart, like the wings of a bird, subsided.

Each day she'd sought him out, attempting to comfort him by telling him stories that provided him with the hope of freedom, and the child clung to her. Deep bonds were formed between Helena and the boy.

Every day in the camp was precarious, but Adam's need of her strengthened her determination to survive.

Helena knew that the yellow star attached to the jacket that

Adam wore could put him in mortal danger. So, when a Gypsy child died in the barracks, she exchanged Adam's jacket with that of the dead child, trusting that this might help him survive. However, in the early hours of one cold and grey morning Adam was torn away from Helena when he was transported out of the camp together with a truckload of children. Helena, bereft, was convinced that she would never see him again.

Gently Helena urged Adam to tell his story.

"What happened to you from the time you left Auschwitz, until you were liberated?" she asked. At her prodding, his expression became closed; he clamped his jaw shut and turned away. Helena and Rachel knew to ask him no more.

After liberation, many of the children who had survived were sent by ship to Palestine and as fate played its mysterious hand, Adam was placed on the same kibbutz as the one Helena was on.

"It will be my thirteenth birthday soon and I will be celebrating my bar mitzvah on the kibbutz," he said yawning sleepily before his eyelids drooped and he fell asleep with his head buried in the crook of Helena's arm.

Soon after this encounter, Adam was claimed by relatives of his mother who lived in England and had been searching for him. Before he left the kibbutz and to the heartfelt joy of every resident, the authorities brought Adam the news that his mother had survived and that soon they would be reunited.

However, the bond that developed between Adam and Helena in Auschwitz would last throughout their lives.

Once Rachel's talents as a cook were discovered she was put in charge of the kitchen, while Helena's knowledge of English and her administrative skills saw her again being put to work in the office. Helena's youthful beauty had not gone unnoticed by the single, ardent men on the kibbutz and these eager young fellows made many attempts at wooing her. But it was only friendship that Helena sought from them. When she lit her Sabbath candles it was Max's face that appeared in the flame and only his love that she yearned for. She continued to cling to the hope that he would fulfil his promise and meet with her in Palestine.

Chapter 23

1948

It was early morning on the kibbutz, the air still cool. But as a golden orb of sun broke through the horizon into a solid blue sky, it brought with it the promise of another brutally hot day.

For now, a breeze whispered through the branches of the tall trees in the orange grove. Helena lingered along the path on her way to the administration office, enjoying the shade and the smell of oranges that permeated the air. Soon the coolness would be only a memory as the heat settled in, beating down on the roof of the office in which she worked.

A rustling sound in the tree above stopped her in her track and she looked up. Two deeply-tanned legs slithered down the trunk of the tree, and a girl with a bag of oranges strapped to her back plopped down to the ground in front of her. Startled, Helena jumped backwards, stifling a scream.

"Wh- who are you?" she stammered.

The figure crouching on the ground stood up, dusted herself down and held out a strong tanned hand.

"I didn't mean to scare you. My name is Ruth Weiss."

Helena found herself staring at an elfin face split by a broad smile that displayed perfect white teeth. A pair of clear, wide-set hazel eyes looked back at her. Ruth ran her fingers through her dark closely-cropped hair.

"I have been picking oranges this morning. This harvest is the best," she said, bending to gather the oranges that had rolled out of her bag. Straightening up, she held one out to Helena.

"What is your name?" she asked.

"Helena, but you can call me Lenie." Helena smiled as she held out both hands to receive the orange. When Ruth noticed the tattooed prisoner number on the inside of Helena's arm, it was her turn to be shocked. Her smile disappeared and her eyes clouded over.

"Are you a survivor?" she asked cautiously, fighting back tears. When Helena lowered her head in acknowledgment, Ruth spontaneously threw her arms around her.

"Oh, little one, it's a miracle that you are here." A sob broke through her voice. Then she linked her arm through Helena's. Sharing the weight of the bag of oranges, the two women made their way through the grove towards the office.

"Tell me about yourself," Ruth said.

Helena was intrigued by Ruth's strange, slightly guttural accent, so different to her ear.

"Where are you from?" she asked, before answering her question. "I have not heard your accent before."

Ruth threw back her head and laughed from deep within her throat.

"I am from South Africa. My home is in Paarl, a scenic country town set in the winelands on the outskirts of Cape Town. It has huge, old oak trees lining the streets, and vineyards heavy with bunches of purple grapes are seen throughout the town during the summer months. In spring the jacaranda trees shed their flowers and create a lilac shower that carpet the streets.

My parents live there and own a small grocery store. I came to Israel to offer my assistance to this kibbutz but my parents are elderly, and I will have to return home soon."

"I hope not too soon." Helena smiled shyly at her, tightening her grip on Ruth's arm.

By the time Helena and Ruth reached the administration office, a friendship that would endure throughout their lives had been formed. The tale of how Ruth fell out of the orange tree and landed at Helena's feet would be recounted with peals of laughter many times in the future, long after Ruth had returned to South Africa to marry her childhood sweetheart, Jonathan Meyer, and to help her parents in their grocery store. Despite the distance between them and the years they would spend apart, Ruth and Helena's friendship would continue to strengthen.

The appearance of Ruth on the kibbutz wove a colourful thread into the lives of Helena and Rachel. Ruth's startling outspokenness set Rachel off laughing as her heart warmed to the tomboyish South African.

The death of Sofia, her beloved childhood friend, continued to cast a dark cloud over Helena's world. Each Sabbath, as they stood before the lit candles, Rachel saw Helena's lips tremble as she recited the prayer to welcome the Sabbath. Helena would press her fingers against her eyes, recalling Sofia's face in the flame of the candles. Sofia had been her only connection to her family, her life in Poland and the culture it represented, and she was overwhelmed with so much loss.

Ruth's friendship had a healing effect on Helena. After

meeting Ruth in the orange orchard, it was as though she regained some of her youth. She and Ruth pored over magazines they salvaged from visitors to the kibbutz. They discussed the latest movie stars and fashion trends as they styled each other's hair. Ruth made a game of holding out a magazine depicting a female movie star in front of her. With her other hand to the back of her head, she swayed her hips and strutted about, pouting her lips in a parody of the actress. Rachel would double up, choked with laughter, until they all collapsed in a heap of hilarity.

Rachel observed this new lightness about Helena as the two girls spend all their recreational time together. Gazing at Helena and Ruth, their arms intertwined, their laughter mingling, she became pensive.

Helena is a delicate bloom, she thought, *that should have been nurtured in the warmth of the sun. Instead, she was placed in the teeth of a storm.* Remembering the suffering that she and Helena had endured sent shafts of pain stabbing at her. *And yet,* she thought, her spirits lifting, *we are alive.* She marvelled at their resilience and in that one blissful moment, Rachel experienced the triumph of survival and the miracle of life.

It was the end of another day on the kibbutz and the last of the afternoon rays were dissolving into dusk. Cascading sparks from the campfire illuminated the darkening sky. The residents of the kibbutz were gathered around the fire preparing their evening meal. The bedtime songs of the children drifted towards them and they smiled at the sweetness of the voices. The woody smell of the fire mingled with that of toasted pita bread lathered with goatmilk cheese.

Sitting close to the fire, Ruth turned to Rachel and Helena.

"I will be returning to South Africa sometime soon," she said, licking the last of the runny cheese from her fingers.

Helena looked crestfallen.

"When do you plan to leave?" she asked, her glum expression revealing more than her words did.

Between bites of pita bread, Ruth spoke of her love for her childhood sweetheart, Jonathan Meyer.

"We plan to marry next summer when he graduates from the University of Cape Town." She wiped the last crumbs from her hands. "But I am sure that you and I will maintain our close ties even though we'll be living so far apart. You have come to mean so much to me, both of you."

She stretched out her hands to take one each of Rachel's and Helena's.

"Your friendship has been my gift and the memories thereof will follow me back to South Africa."

Clasping hands, the friends nodded in agreement. They remained sitting there until the flames burned low, the fireflies pricked the night sky with their light and the crickets began their song.

When Helena spoke to Ruth of her love for Max, Rachel noted the soulful look in her eyes. Helena had obstinately clung to the belief that Max would meet her in Palestine as he promised he would when they were in Berlin. The absence of letters or any communication from him since they arrived at the Blums' home in Paris, had left Rachel doubtful that Max would keep to his word. She turned away lest Helena see the sorrow in her eyes.

Were Rachel able to guess at the events that were about to unfold, events that would change the course of their lives, her sorrow would have turned to joy.

The days cooled down as winter approached, bringing developments that would forever impact on the lives of the inhabitants of Palestine. History was about to be made. The United Nations had agreed to a vote on a resolution that would create a Jewish state, thereby realising a dream for the survivors, pioneers and the entire Jewish population globally.

On the day of the voting, the apprehension was palpable. Crowds gathered at dusk in the town square where loudspeakers had been set up. Tremors of anticipation rippled through the crowd as the world held its collective breath, awaiting the outcome. When the gavel announced the conclusion, loudspeakers and hailers informed the tense crowd that the resolution had been adopted and the new State of Israel had been born.

People embraced each another, shedding joyous tears. As the news spread, the elated crowds grew bigger and, swept up in the moment, they danced and sang throughout the night. *Hatikvah*, the anthem previously banned by the British, was sung with gusto and Rachel and Helena were among the most joyful of the revellers.

On this memorable night sleep was not an option. Tomorrow they would deal with their daily duties and the exhaustion that a sleepless night was sure to bring. Tonight, after thousands of years of wandering, the Jews finally had a home of their own.

For now, that was all that mattered.

But their joy was short-lived.

Alone in his office, Prime Minister David Ben Gurion remained pensive, listening to the roar of the exulting crowd.

The flickering lamplight cast a dancing silhouette against the wall and illuminated his features etched with lines of worry. His heart was heavy. War clouds were looming and he acknowledged that the fragile new State of Israel was ill equipped for an onslaught. Britain, hoping to maintain control, had handed tanks and weapons to the Arab states to be used against Israel and they had destroyed much-needed hospital equipment. Israel was surrounded by hostile states.

Predictably, the moment independence was declared, the Prime Minister's worst fears were realised and the surrounding Arab nations declared war – a war to be waged by an enraged Goliath against a diminutive David.

The news of the declaration of war in the Middle East quickly spread across the globe. Men and women of all ages and nationalities, with little or no experience but determined to assist the Jewish State and end the bitter conflict, boarded flights for the fledgling State of Israel.

Chapter 24

NEW YORK

WINTER 1948

Evening stretched across the sky, the late afternoon sun burnishing the New York skyline into muted shades of crimson and gold. Max Harris's luxury sedan purred as he cruised along the highway headed for home. It had been a long and exhausting day in court, his case hard won.

He hummed tunelessly along with the background music coming from the radio, his fingers drumming the beat against the steering wheel. He relished the sensation of having loosened his collar and the knot of his tie, and mentally replayed the day's events. When he remembered his dinner date with friends, arranged by Jenny for later that evening, he felt his tension ebb away.

Abruptly the music stopped. The announcer's voice cut in on the programme, jolting Max out of his daydream. The urgency in the announcer's voice was unmistakable.

"We interrupt this programme to make an important announcement. War has broken out in the Middle East. The newly-formed State of Israel is at war with its neighbours."

Stunned by the announcement, Max pulled over to the side of the highway. He listened attentively to the details accompanying the appalling news that filtered through the airwaves. Caught in a mesh of turbulent emotions, he sat hunched behind the steering wheel absorbing the news. The impact of the announcement caused him to lose all sense of time. When he finally collected his thoughts, he had made an irreversible decision. He started the car engine to continue on his route, but it felt as though the world had shifted on its axis.

After making a few phone calls and throwing some belongings together, he explained to Yetta and Jenny as gently as possible his decision to leave for Israel the following day to help with the war effort. The furore that took place when he broke the news was expected.

Yetta cried and clung to him, beseeching him not to go. But when she recognised the determined set of his jaw and realised that her tears were in vain, she turned to the mantelpiece. Lifting the silver candlesticks belonging to Samuel's mother, which she had carried from their home in Russia, she thrust them at Max.

"Take them, my son. They will be your protection as they were for your father." She sobbed, her tears drenching Max's shirt as she held him close.

Jenny's tears, however, were tears of rage. Her blue eyes turned icy as she stared at Max, refusing to believe that he would abandon her for a world so far removed from their opulent lifestyle. Her cajoling had no effect and in a fit of rage, she flung her engagement ring at Max's feet and stormed out of the apartment.

Yetta looked on in horror, but it surprised Max that the feeling that surged through him as he stared at Jenny's receding back was one of relief. He gathered Yetta in his arms, rocking her gently as though she were a child.

"It's going to be all right, Mamma. This is what is meant to be. Have faith in me and we will be stronger once we are reunited after the war," he said as he soothed her.

Dinner that night was a solemn affair with just Yetta, Gloria and Max seated around the dinner table. Sitting at the head of the table, Max turned to his mother and sister.

"I shall never forget all that I witnessed in Berlin after the war. Because of that, I feel compelled to fight for our homeland so that the atrocities I was exposed to can never be repeated. This is a mission I must fulfil and there is a promise I need to keep."

Sitting on either side of Max, Yetta and Gloria each clasped one of his hands and nodded sombrely. The trio, drawn together by deep bonds of love, continued their meal.

By morning Max was gone.

Since she arrived on the shores of America carrying her mother-in-law's silver candlesticks, Yetta never regretted her decision to marry Samuel Harris and to follow him to this far-distant land about which she knew so little. But then, she would have followed Samuel to the end of the earth. She loved him then as she revered his memory now.

Yetta had witnessed many changes to her life in the years after her marriage, as she stood firmly and stoically beside Samuel supporting him in all his decisions. At times, she allowed her mind to drift back to the past as she recalled the first years of their marriage.

They set up home in Brooklyn. At night Samuel would sit beside the table in their rented room, which was lit by the light of the candles placed in the silver candlesticks, his few dollars spread on the table before him. Every cent was allocated for their daily needs. A bus trip was a luxury. Samuel had come to America with only a few dollars in his pocket, but a big dream in his heart and an unwavering resolve to realise it.

He had a good head for business. Samuel was also generous and loving by nature. When Miller Harris Furnishers began to thrive, he took pleasure in showering his family with the rewards of his success. Yetta had placed her faith in her solid and dependable Samuel, and she never regretted it.

Max's sudden departure to help fight the war in Israel brought another change to her life, one she would have to face alone. Throughout their marriage Samuel had praised her for the spirited way in which she overcame obstacles but now a chill came over her, leaving her feeling hollow, insecure and fearful for Max's safety.

It is the morning after Max's departure. Yetta wandered listlessly about the elegant apartment. The clamour of the traffic in the street far below drifted towards her. The smell of rain was in the air. Distracted, her gaze strayed to the portrait of Samuel displayed on the mantelpiece. She lifted it and held it up to the morning light which streamed in through the windows.

Oh Sam, how I miss you. How will I bear the emptiness that Max has brought to my life by leaving, without having you to guide me?

She continued to speak to the portrait, suppressing a spasm of fear, but the image of Samuel Harris which captured his younger years, stared mutely back at her.

Yetta continued her conversation with Samuel's portrait. *He is a good boy, our Max, so much like his father ...* She smiled at the thought, and tears welled in her eyes. *He is determined and strong-willed and radiates life but like you, Sam, he is steadfast in his principles and sets himself high goals.*

The ringing of the doorbell broke into her musings. The housekeeper opened the door and Gloria swept into the apartment, enveloped in a cloud of expensive perfume, sparking energy. Flinging aside her leather handbag she embraced Yetta.

"Mamma, it will not bring you any comfort to remain in the apartment on your own today worrying about Max. I have booked a table for lunch with friends at the Savoy and you must join us. There is heavy traffic to navigate so we need to hurry."

Yetta smoothed the sides of her silver-grey hair with perfectly-manicured hands and tugged at the hem of her cream-coloured wool jacket, preparing to leave. As Gloria ushered her towards the door, Yetta looked back over her shoulder at Samuel's portrait once more.

Speaking aloud, her Russian accent tinged with a pleasing Brooklyn lilt, she said, "We have good children, Samuel. They are your greatest achievement."

Then the door closed firmly behind her.

Chapter 25

ISRAEL

WINTER 1947-1949

With the commencement of war, the residents of the kibbutz were fraught with despair. Haifa was a strategic port. Planes tore across the skies sending shivers of fear through the residents, while a symphony of sirens screeching warnings of imminent danger sent them scuttling to their shelters. News filtered through of a lack of planes and manpower, causing further apprehension. No one doubted that it would take a miracle for Israel to win this war, only now they would fight back. This time would be different.

The members of the kibbutz had been secretly trained by the Haganah military who had moved in swiftly to help the residents. Stashed weapons had been hidden on the kibbutz, out of sight of the British who had prohibited the settlers from arming themselves against the Arab nations. Helena had taken part in the training and was proud of her ability to handle these weapons.

Before sunrise, she lay cushioned in the dewy grass, on her morning duty. She held a gun firmly in her hand with her finger poised on the trigger. Edie's words spoken so long ago in Paris echoed in her memory: "You are no longer a victim. Now it is your turn to fight back." And this time she knew she would.

She cocked the gun and squinted into the distance, her ears pricked up for any unwelcome sound and her eyes scanning for movement.

In the still morning air, as the first rays of sun lit up the sky, she remembered another sunrise, one when she was at the mercy of the Nazis.

It was near the end of the war and the Germans were becoming desperate. Their wounded soldiers needed blood transfusions. A ready supply of blood was available to these soldiers from the remnants of the emaciated, barely-living Jews left in the camp. Having their blood drained meant certain death for the frail and malnourished inmates.

When the early morning call came for the inmates to line up outside, Helena, aware of what the commandos were about to do, remained in her bunk scarcely daring to breathe with the fear of being discovered.

Her eyes were clenched shut when she felt the prod of the German soldier's baton.

"Why are you not outside?" he enquired, peering down at her.

"I have typhus," whispered Helena.

The soldier bent down and put a hand to her cool forehead. Although she no longer believed in miracles, she felt one unfolding before her. He gazed at her cynically for a heart-stopping moment before he turned his back and walked away, leaving her lying safely in the bunk.

A sound in the bushes behind her broke through her daydream. Her intense training had taught her to react swiftly. Now all her instincts were alert, and she swung around squeezing the trigger in the direction of the sound. A dull thud in the bushes followed her single shot. Moving stealthily through the undergrowth she discovered the intruder, German guns strewn about his lifeless body.

Helena thought, *I have survived, for this moment. No longer will my people be persecuted and hidden away in ghettos. Now we can defend ourselves openly. We have taken back our power and we will never be defeated again.*

She heard footsteps running towards her. She sprung around, aiming her gun once more, but relief washed over her as she recognised the soldiers from the kibbutz. They had heard the gunshot and rushed to her aid. These soldiers were on their way to Lebanon and had stopped over at the kibbutz for a warm meal and a comfortable bed.

They were astonished at Helena's deftness in handling a dangerous situation and they heaped praise on her. The German guns collected from the intruder were gratefully received and added to the stash already on the kibbutz.

The steely look in Helena's eyes and the proud set of her shoulders reflected the feeling of strength with which this incident had empowered her.

Chapter 26

ISRAEL

WINTER 1948-1949

Rachel could be found daily in the makeshift kitchen that had been set up by the residents. Her back and shoulders were curled around as she stood at the wooden table vigorously buttering mounds of sliced bread that would be turned into sandwiches for the long line of soldiers at the kitchen door. Her working overalls were covered by a voluminous white apron, her hair tied back with a white kerchief.

Her chest swelled with pride as the soldiers returned for more sandwiches and each one was greeted with a playful and wide-eyed, "More, *Schatzi*?"

But her lips moved continuously in silent prayer as explosions rattled the walls of the kitchen.

Every member of the kibbutz contributed to help the war situation. While Rachel had undertaken to keep the soldiers fed, Helena once again found herself in an administrative position in the office. After her early morning lookout duty, she kept account of the uniforms and ammunition being allocated to the soldiers and newly-arrived volunteers.

As she handed out the parcels, she too murmured a prayer

for the safety of each of the soldiers in the snaking queue leading up to her office.

"Miss, do you have my name in your ledger?" asked a soldier at the front of the queue. The sound of his voice startled her. Her breath caught in her throat and her heart darted about.

Her head was bowed low over the ledger and her voice barely audible when she asked, "What is your name?"

"Max Harris from New York. I am a volunteer," he replied.

Hearing his voice peeled back the layers of time, exposing the throbbing ache in her heart. Helena looked up into Max's eyes and their worlds collided.

He looked older, his features drawn but more clearly defined. Only the gentleness in his eyes fringed with heavy lashes, remained unchanged. As recognition dawned it was as though Max was struck by a lightning bolt. He felt his throat clench. He stood perfectly still absorbing every detail of her: the pulse that throbbed in the base of her smooth, pale throat; the arch of her eyebrows; the way the light caught the delicate bones of her face and he knew that he would remember this moment forever.

Leaning forward he cradled her face in his hands. His lips trembling with emotion, he murmured, "Helena, I have found you." The he stepped around the table and folded her into his arms. "Fate has helped us find each other. We have defied time and distance; this is our destiny, our miracle. We will win this war for our children and grandchildren. Nothing will separate us again."

He held her so close that she could feel his heart beat and taste the salt of his tears.

Max and Helena stood wrapped in the jubilation of their

love, oblivious of their surroundings. The men waiting next in line were enthralled at the tenderness of the scene they were witnessing and broke into a roar of approval. Amidst the clapping, jest and merriment, the fate of Max and Helena was forever sealed.

PART THREE

1990

Chapter 27

ISRAEL

Helena sits at her desk. The envelope and its contents that lie on the desk tug at her, enticing her to take a closer look, but memories come rushing in. Deep in thought, she removes her spectacles, slowly cleaning the lenses with a handkerchief before replacing them.

Behind her Rachel reclines in an armchair. The dying rays of the afternoon sun bathe her with a lucent light. Her hands resting on the covers are as dry and veined as autumn leaves, the toll of the years evident on her wrinkled brow.

Helena turns around, her gaze lingering on Rachel. She smiles when she sees how peacefully she dozes in the sun. She wonders: *When did Rachel's hair become so white?* Her eyes settle on the mantelpiece upon which stand the silver candlesticks that once belonged to Samuel's grandmother and then his mother. Yetta carried these candlesticks from Samuel's home in Russia to New York, and their son, Max, brought them to Israel.

There is a mirror positioned between the candlesticks in which she catches her own reflection. The light is softer now, more forgiving, and yet she sees the silver threads weaving through her fair hair and the fine lines etched in her face, deeper now since the accident.

Helena has looped her curls at the nape of her neck, but one fair strand of hair has escaped, winding down the side of her neck. Distractedly she tugs at it, coiling it around a finger. Then a thought strikes her: it was her fair hair and blue eyes that played a significant role in her survival during the war. She covers her eyes with her hands as memories like shadows flicker behind her lids and she is transported back to the Poland of her childhood in 1939.

Within days of invading Poland, the new Nazi laws were applied to the Jewish residents of all the surrounding towns. In the Jablonski home, as in all the Jewish homes, a night curfew came into effect and food rationing was imposed on them. The rations barely covered the family's needs and obtaining food on the black market became a source of survival. Bread was almost unobtainable.

Wiktor was a policeman who worked in the town and had formed a friendly alliance with the Jablonski family. When skirmishes broke out at Tateh's leather factory he would intervene on Tateh's behalf, restoring calm. In turn, Tateh supplied Wiktor and his family with new leather shoes and mended the worn ones.

When the curfew was imposed, and all Jews were forced to wear armbands with yellow stars attached to them, Wiktor was outraged at the indignity heaped upon his Jewish friends. Each evening he would call at the Jablonski home. He concluded that Helena's blonde curls and blue eyes would help her pass as his daughter. He would regularly remove her armband, take her hand and walk her safely through the streets to his home before nightfall. They successfully evaded the ever-watchful Nazi soldiers wandering the streets, who were intent on their sinister mission of inflicting harm on any Jew seen on the street after curfew. Warm loaves of fresh bread awaited Helena at Wiktor's home, and she would carry these back to her anguished family with Wiktor as protection by her side.

Turning back to the desk, her gaze settles on the framed photographs arranged around it. She remains motionless, lost in the memories of the past. The largest one, the black and white photograph of her marriage to Max leaps out at her, their joy in each other caught by the eye of the camera and frozen in time.

They were married on the kibbutz once the war was won and hostilities ended. Pierre and Edie flew in from Paris, together with Jacques and Amelie. They embraced Rachel and Helena, vying for their attention, their words tumbling together in their pleasure at being reunited. They beamed when Helena introduced them to her handsome groom, and showered Max with the same love they had for Rachel and Helena.

Yetta and Gloria arrived from New York. All Yetta's misgivings about the ending of Max's relationship with Jenny were quelled the moment she met Helena.

"My, ain't she pretty?" Yetta purred, holding Helena at arm's length to admire her.

Gloria, too, was drawn to the serenity of this guileless young girl. Helena glowed with the abundance of love and admiration showered on her.

Their throats tightened and they were unable to speak when they noticed the tattoo on her inner forearm. It made them even more determined to draw Helena close into the security of their family circle. Max, observing his mother and Helena embrace each other with their heads bowed together in earnest conversation, felt a surge of love for both of them. He murmured a prayer of gratitude for the journey that had brought him to this moment.

It was a sparkling day, their wedding day. The sky was an unblemished canopy that stretched to the horizon until it merged with the ocean. Helena's fragile beauty was enhanced by the simple white dress she wore. Rachel had sewn the dress from a bolt of white fabric intended for kitchen uniforms. Skilfully she had created an elegant wedding gown, stitching panels that flowed gently to the hemline from the V-shaped neckline, emphasising Helena's petiteness. A garland of white daisies woven by Ruth held a gossamer veil in place, completing the picture of a serene and beautiful bride.

Rachel, her arm threaded through Helena's, walked her towards the wedding canopy where Max waited for his bride. His eyes shone with love as she circled around him seven times, radiant in her beauty. When the vows were completed under the canopy, the rabbi indicated to Ruth, who stood at Helena's side, to lift her veil. Rachel passed a goblet of wine to Helena for her to sip from. There were smiles and laughter when Max slipped a plain, gold band on Helena's finger and then stepped on a glass covered in a cloth, breaking it, and the ceremony was concluded.

How tenuous is the world we inhabit and how transient
our joy ... the symbolic connotation of the breaking of
a glass, proved to be prophetic for Max and Helena.

The celebration culminated in a sumptuous feast that was shared by every member of the kibbutz, including the ageing and portly rabbi who had married Max and Helena. He joined in the singing and danced energetically. He refilled his wine glass just as energetically until at last he collapsed into a chair, his snores competing with the singing. Yetta and Gloria kicked off their stilettos and danced together with the wedding party until late into the night.

A shimmering star-packed Milky Way suspended in an inky-black sky signalled the end of a perfect day. Holding hands while running through a shower of rose petals, a shooting star lit up the heavens. Max and Helena felt as though they would live forever.

As the last of the wedding guests trailed off to their cabins for a night's rest, a feeling of peace descended on the kibbutz. It had been a joyous celebration and the inhabitants and guests had been delighted to witness the union of this young and loving couple. It was as though the angels had orchestrated this marriage and joined their celestial chorus with that of the well-wishers.

Alone in their cabin at last, Max drew Helena to him and

unpinned her curls, letting her hair tumble about her shoulders. He felt her stiffen at his touch as she had in the past, recoiling at the suggestion of any contact more intimate than a few kisses. But Max understood, and he was patient. He was aware that because of her experiences in the camp the physical touch of a man brought with it the dread and fear of pain and degradation. He felt the tremors pass down her spine.

He took a deep breath and placed his palms on either side of her face, tilting it up towards him. He gazed into the depths of her eyes.

"Helena, how I wish that I could blot out all the pain and suffering that you have endured these past years, but I cannot. What I can do is to promise to love you with all my heart and protect you with all my body for all the days that I spend with you. Please trust me."

Eyes brimming with love gazed back at him through lashes moist with tears. He felt her body soften as she leaned towards him, her arms reaching around his back, her heart beating close to his. Tenderly he slipped her nightgown over her bare shoulders, the moon bathing her pale skin with its golden glow.

Morning had crept onto the windowsill when a thrush in full throttle alighted on it. He hopped from one foot to another in an attempt to draw the attention of the couple sleeping on the bed beneath the window. Cocking his head, he gazed quizzically at their contented, ethereal faces and tangled limbs twisted in the bedclothes, their arms thrown loosely around each other.

When increasing his volume still had no effect on the sleeping couple, the thrush turned around, fluffed out his feathers and headed off to the branch of the nearest tree to continue his solitary morning song.

The day after the wedding, Yetta and Gloria returned to New York and the Blums and Lamonts returned to Paris. But for Max and Helena, wrapped in the warmth of a world of their own, the euphoria of their wedding day was enduring. They delighted in each other as they learned their ways. Just a touch on her arm from Max when passing, or his lopsided smile when she used an English word out of context with her pronounced Polish accent, was enough to fill Helena with love for him.

Many weeks had passed since their wedding day. It was morning. The first downy rays of the sun filtered through the bedroom window, sweeping away the night's dark shadows. Max turned to Helena, asleep in the bed beside him. The silvery light dappled the skin of her bare back and shoulders as though the windswept stars had left their imprint. He marvelled at her seductive beauty and listened to her even breathing, knowing that their love would last until the end of time.

Helena's eyes fluttered open. She lay still for a moment as the fogginess of sleep dissolved. When wakefulness dawned, a smile broke inside her and she nudged into the warm curve of Max's body. He kissed the softness in the nape of her neck and rejoiced that there were still hours stretching ahead of them before the start of another working day. And yet the moments they spent together never seemed enough.

There were times when Helena heard the voice of her father in the rush of the wind and her mother's voice in birdsong. But in moments such as these, when it felt as though time stood still, she sensed their presence most.

"Be happy my child," her mother would whisper. "Our love for you is bound up with that of Max's."

If there is a heaven, Helena would think, *and they are in it, I know that they are smiling down on me.*

There would yet be many demons for Helena to face, but her battle to conquer them would be fought with Max at her side.

Chapter 28

ISRAEL
1950-1955

Helena and Max settled down quietly as the weeks passed and life returned to a daily routine. In order to pursue his legal career, Max bought a spacious house in Jerusalem with a large shady garden in the front. Rachel, forever Helena's North Star, shared their home. She glowed with pride as she observed Helena's metamorphosis since her marriage to Max ... like a butterfly breaking out of a chrysalis. For Rachel, the security of a home and routine gave her a sense of belonging, filling a deep need in her and allowing her to begin the slow process of healing.

But still, in unguarded moments, Rachel and Helena would turn to each other and see the pain reflected in their eyes, and the fragile shells of their worlds would splinter and crack as deeply-buried memories broke through.

Rachel had kept her promise, and headstones for her family and Sofia had been consecrated in the Jerusalem cemetery. On days when thoughts of her beloved family overwhelmed her, she would go to the cemetery and place a traditional small white stone at the foot of each of their headstones. Standing there, she would release her anguish and grief. It rose up inside her in waves until she howled her rage in heaving gulps into the throbbing silence and solitude of her surroundings. She wept a torrent of tears for the lives that were stolen from her young sons and from every member of her close-knit family.

What was all this death and destruction about?

The agonising question caused the bitter taste of bile to rise in her throat. Was it all brought about on the whim of a small, moustached and deranged man, Adolf Hitler? Her only answer was the mocking silence from the surrounding graves. Then, depleted of emotion, Rachel would garner her inner strength and head for home, a home in which she was ensconced with the love of Max and Helena. She found solace in knowing that her family would be immortalised in Yad Vashem.

Rachel coaxed Helena to enrol at a university and with Max's support, she registered for a teaching degree. Helena's studies proved challenging, but her developing love of teaching children encouraged her to persevere. Her graduation was a moment of triumph and a celebration of her achievement. She had fulfilled the pledge she had made to Edie in Paris that she would rebuild her life, availing herself of every opportunity. Max and Rachel were flushed with pride as they watched Helena being capped by the rector of the university.

Helena took up a teaching post, through which she came to guide and define the lives of many young students who loved her and respected her discipline. About a year after she had started teaching at a nursery school, she met Gerda Halperin and a friendship was formed that only a few years before Helena would not have thought possible.

After classes the children scattered, eager to get home. All but little Doron Halperin, who waited for his mother Gerda to collect him at the classroom door where Helena would hand him over to her. There was something different about Gerda. Although she wore the traditional headscarf and long sleeves of an observant Jewish woman, there was something vaguely familiar or reminiscent of the past ... Helena tried engaging her in conversation, but Gerda always averted her eyes and, taking Doron's hand, would hurry away.

Then one day this changed. Gerda and Doron had reached the school gate when Gerda turned around. Walking back up the pathway, she approached Helena.

"*Morah* Lenie, I have noticed the tattoo on your arm. Are you a survivor of the Nazi concentration camps?" she asked.

Taken by surprise, Helena nodded.

Gerda's face appeared to crumple and she reached out and gingerly touched the tattoo on Helena's arm.

"Before I married, my name was Gerda Kranz. I am the daughter of German citizens and my father was a Nazi officer during the war."

Shocked at hearing Gerda's words, Helena felt a pulse begin to throb in her temple and instinctively took a step backwards. She covered her mouth with her hand, her eyes wide with horror.

Prompted by Helena's reaction, Gerda continued her story.

"During the war I lived with my parents in Berlin and worked as a secretary until I became aware of the atrocities being carried out by the Nazis, including my father who was in the Wehrmacht. I left home and Germany and managed to reach England where I found work as a nanny. I have not seen either of my parents again. We became just another family torn apart by the trauma of war. I married into a Jewish family. My husband is very caring and understood my dilemma.

"I studied hard to become an Orthodox Jewess. It wasn't easy but I had the support of my new family who encouraged me to graduate. Now the entire family has come to settle in Israel."

She looked up into Helena's shocked eyes.

"How can you ever forgive me? But on behalf of my people, I ask for forgiveness."

Seeing the pain in Gerda's eyes, the throbbing in Helena's temples subsided and she became calm. She weighed her words carefully before answering, "We were both innocent children who were drawn into a war we had nothing to do with. The legacy that your father has left both of us with, is that of guilt. You bear the guilt of your nation, while I bear the guilt of having survived while my loved ones did not. Should we become friends it might not lessen the guilt but will hopefully help us to heal and to accept that over which we had no control."

A tenuous but cathartic friendship was formed that day that with time and many tears would become an enduring one, piecing together the broken parts of each of their lives. They discovered that guilt was burdensome and unsustainable and that ultimately only love endures. Their friendship became a beacon of light that steered them through what had been the darkest days of their lives.

While Helena was embarking on her career, Max's professional life was gathering steam. He had passed the required legal bar exam in Jerusalem and was articled to a highly-regarded firm of lawyers. His logical mind and controversial views caught the attention of the partners of the firm as well as that of politicians. There were broad smiles and much back-slapping the day he was made a partner of the firm Solomon, Gorsky and Harris, and his air-conditioned corner office was soon inundated with clients seeking his legal advice.

It was Max, her soulmate, who swelled with pride at her accomplishments, and it was Max her friend and lover who held her through the long nights until the haunting voices of her murdered family and the cries of starving children were silenced, until the tremors subsided. It was Max, her refuge, who left behind a deep, dark void when he too was gone. And it was the loss of Max, her only love, that burdened her with the weight of sorrow.

Chapter 29

Helena's spirits lift as her gaze shifts to the photograph of their twins, Ilan and Orit, as teenagers. The laughter in their eyes, so like Max's, is clearly visible. Her pride in them makes her heart swell. Being Sabras, they are independent and resourceful and living proof to their parents of Hitler's defeat. This brave young generation heralds the rebirth of a nation and is a source of hope and pride to the survivors in their fragile new homeland.

The moment that the twins entered the world signalled the pinnacle of Helena's happiness. As the babies took their first breath, they were placed on her chest, their tiny hearts beating against hers. She cradled the babies, stroking their soft, downy heads. She saw the shape of her father's nose in Ilan's and her mother's eyes in Orit's.

It is for these children that I have survived, Helena thought, floating on a cloud of euphoria. *During the lonely years of longing for my family and of hunger and deprivation I could not have imagined that this moment would be possible.*

As she surrendered to drowsiness she murmured a prayer for her babies: *May their days be anointed with the morning dew and their evenings be crowned with a sunset.*

How easily Helena recaptures the vision of a beaming Max, an infant tucked into the crook of each arm, introducing the children to an enraptured Rachel whose love for these children would enrich their lives. Throughout their childhood, it would be the steaming bowls of broth and the comfort of her lap to which Ilan and Orit would be drawn. It was Rachel's welcoming arms that awaited them when they returned from classes while their parents worked.

The scent of warm apples and cinnamon drifting from Rachel's apple strudel filled the kitchen and nourished their souls as well as their bodies.

When Dr Levy delivered the twins, he observed the prisoner number tattooed on the inside of Helena's arm. He stood at her bedside and taking her hand, looked deeply into her eyes.

"Helena, I can remove the tattoo for you if you will allow me to," he said.

Helena remained contemplative. All too clearly, she remembered the pain and indignity of receiving the tattoo in Auschwitz and the humiliation of having her identity reduced to a number.

The pain of childbirth was a different pain, one to be exalted. The birth of the twins reinforced her identity as a strong and independent woman and the mother of a new generation.

With characteristic determination, she lifted her chin and answered with an emphatic, "No."

Max, standing beside the bed, appeared incredulous.

"Why, Lenie? Why not accept the doctor's kind offer and blot out the past?"

Helena's reply was firm. "The time will come when there will be denial of what happened to the Jews in the Holocaust. I have to bear the burden of proof."

Dr Levy and Max both tightened their grip on her hands in acknowledgement; words were superfluous.

Helena, Max and Rachel returned to the kibbutz to introduce their babies to the residents. A feast had been laid out to welcome these two little Sabras into the kibbutz family. Chocolate and cheesecakes, pita bread, falafel and an assortment of salads were among the delicacies offered to these special guests. Little children danced and sang, encircling the babies who lay gurgling contentedly in their proud parents' arms.

The months and years passed by and Orit and Ilan emerged from babyhood into childhood. As the twins grew, Orit was clearly the feistier of the two and she tended to make her desires known. She would cock her hip, place her hand on her waist and toss her head in a stance so reminiscent of Eva, that Helena would have to blink away the spectre of her little sister hovering behind Orit.

Time elapsed and Orit and Ilan grew into vibrant and energetic children. They were a common sight on the kibbutz, spending all their school holidays there. They flourished in the fresh open air, running around freely with the other children and learning the stories of their land. Orit could always be found among the fluffy yellow chicks in the henhouse or feeding the newly-born lambs, while Ilan trailed behind the mechanics. He was fascinated with the tools they used to fix tractors and engines, and his talent for all things technical soon became evident.

It was among Helena's most enduring memories when she

observed Max engaging with the twins. His work schedule kept him working long hours in his office, but when the twins were on holiday on the kibbutz, he closed his office for a few days to enable him to spend time with his beloved family.

Helena watched them from a distance. Ilan and Max would be immersed in the workings of mechanical gadgets. Sitting cross-legged on the ground, they would take these gadgets apart just to put them together again. Father and son built a go-kart from odd bits of timber and wheels they found in the sheds on the kibbutz. After much hammering and drilling, the cart was completed and Max pushed Ilan, seated in it, down the hill. He ran alongside, both of them whooping into the rushing wind.

The twins had boundless energy. When Max arranged a soccer match for the children on the kibbutz, Helena reluctantly got dragged into the game as a referee. The teams played with gusto, accompanied with raucous shouting and whistle-blowing, until one side claimed victory and the sun set on the kibbutz.

Max helped Orit feed the lambs and chicks. He was as gentle with the animals as he was boisterous on the soccer field.

The kibbutz held precious memories for Max, Helena and Rachel and they observed with pride that as their twins thrived, so did the kibbutz.

The rocky, barren soil was replaced with lush green lawns, and brick houses appeared where once wooden cabins had stood. Roses and bougainvillea splashed colour across a landscape that had once been drab and colourless, and the scent of jasmine pervaded the air.

Orit, their fun-loving tomboy daughter, defied convention from an early age. Healing was her passion, and throughout her childhood she carefully tended lame dogs, injured cats and birds in a corner of her bedroom. Max shared her love of animals and kept a watchful eye over them as they recovered. It came as no surprise when, having completed her schooling and a stint in the army, Orit obtained her medical degree and joined a cancer research programme. Nor was it entirely a surprise when she introduced Raquel, a Palestinian research worker on her team, to Max and Helena.

Max, Helena and the two young women were gathered around the kitchen table. Holding hands, Orit and Raquel confided that their friendship had grown into a loving union. Orit leaned across the table, gazing earnestly at her parents, searching their expressions for approval. Max turned to Helena and shrugged his shoulders, his palms upturned.

"Lenie," he said, "it appears that we have another daughter." Hugs were exchanged while they juggled glasses of champagne, and then they all got back to the business of living.

Ilan, their golden boy, stared straight at the camera and into the moment. He had sailed through his schooling, achieving steady A grades. The promise of his younger years was realised and time proved that he had an aptitude for technology. After attaining a university degree, he created a valuable start-up and was head-hunted by a company in Silicon Valley, where he now lived with his wife Debra and young family.

Helena's eyes soften as her gaze rests on the photograph of her cherished grandchildren, Gilad, Sara and baby Benjamin. These children are living proof that her promise to all the fallen souls, that she would perpetuate their legacy, has been fulfilled.

Ilan's dark good looks and tall physique reflected those of his father. However, he had also inherited his mother's blue eyes and gentle ways as well as her steely grit. This became evident when, as an army pilot, he skilfully manoeuvred aircraft in dangerous situations. His family waited anxiously for him to return from each mission but when he did, they shone with pride in their son and brother, resplendent in his pilot's uniform, his cap perched jauntily on his dark curls.

It appeared that Ilan was oblivious to the electrifying effect his good looks had on the myriad of young women who pursued him in his social circle. He courted a series of them and his parents and Rachel were left wondering if he would ever settle down.

It was early afternoon on a Friday and Jerusalem was beginning to shut down for the Sabbath. An aura of peace was settling over the town. Ilan was on his way home from the bus station with his army tote bag slung across his shoulder. Quickening his pace, eager to spend the weekend with his family, he hoisted his tote to the other shoulder. He was looking forward to Rachel's warm apple and cinnamon strudel and thick yoghurt and cucumber salad with falafel balls. He envisaged the bagels boiling in a pot on the stove and the deep-fried potato latkes that he was sure were being prepared for his visit.

A light grey car was parked on the opposite side of the road, its hood raised. An elderly man was bent over the open engine. Ilan noted his agitated expression and the oil smudged across his face and hands, and he crossed the road to where the car was parked.

"Shalom, sir, may I be of help to you?" he asked.

"I-I can't get my car to start, and I need to get home before the Sabbath comes in. I live only a few blocks away." The man straightened up, rubbing his lower back.

Ilan rolled up his sleeves and joined the man, peering into the engine.

"Here is the problem, a wire has come loose," he exclaimed, holding up the broken wire. "I shall have it fixed in no time." The man gave a heavy sigh of relief and patted Ilan's back, grateful for his help.

"Zayde, I have brought you a cup of coffee," a young female voice called out.

Lifting his head from the engine, Ilan's eyes widened and he felt his breathing become shallow as he gazed at the beautiful girl before him who was holding a paper cup in each hand. Her long, jet-black hair was swept off her forehead revealing sparking green eyes set above sculpted cheekbones.

She is so tall, he thought. Caught off guard he stared at her willowy frame. *Almost as tall as I am ...*

Sensing his discomfort, the girl smiled enigmatically as she held out a paper cup to the man. He took the cup from her and turned to Ilan.

"Allow me to introduce myself. I am Ben Leven, and this is my granddaughter, Debra."

Ilan wiped the oil from his hands. "Ilan Harris," he said, locking eyes with Debra. "Your car will start now but let me drive you home. If you live only a few blocks away I can walk home from there."

Gratefully Ben nodded, accepting Ilan's offer. Before climbing into the car Ben turned to Ilan.

"Debra is visiting with me for the weekend. My wife died recently, and she is of great comfort to me. She is a nurse at Hadassah Hospital."

Armed with this information, Ilan cast a sidelong glance at Debra beneath his lashes. The colour rose in her cheeks but she smiled boldly back at him.

In that moment Ilan knew that he had met his match.

Months later, when Ilan announced to his family that he and Debra planned to marry in the summer, they gave the union their blessing and welcomed Debra as joyfully as Raquel had been welcomed.

Once again champagne flowed as the Harris family celebrated the arrival of yet another daughter into their fold.

It is a constant source of sorrow to Helena that Ilan and his family live in another country, so far away from her. How she misses them. She consoles herself with the thought that they will always have a home to come to and they will never have to experience the immense hardship that she had to endure to reach her own homeland. Besides, how keenly she anticipates the visits to Ilan and Debra's home in America, especially since the accident. She and Rachel always receive a rapturous welcome from the children who fling their little arms around their necks, clinging to them and begging for sweet treats and bedtime stories.

The day would come when Rachel and Helena would relate their histories to the children and tell them about the events that brought them to Israel. But not yet. The pure innocence in the children's eyes prevented this and so their stories remained untold, buried deep inside them, secrets that would create a burdensome silence for many generations.

Chapter 30

Helena smiles wistfully as she remembers her first flight to New York, so many years ago.

The twins had just celebrated their first birthdays when Max surprised her with air tickets to New York. He wished to introduce Helena to the rest of the Harris family, whom she had not yet met. Rachel had chosen to remain at home to care for the twins. Helena's childlike excitement at the tumult of the airport beguiled Max, and her apprehension when boarding the plane, the size of which overwhelmed her, endeared her to him. Suppressing a smile, he slipped an arm protectively around her shoulders, drawing her close.

Gloria and Yetta were waiting expectantly at Gloria's Manhattan apartment to welcome them. After her divorce, Gloria had met and married Robert Penn, a New York property developer and architect. She had found the love she craved for herself and her sons in her marriage to Robert.

When Max and Helena arrived at her apartment, Gloria flung open the door to greet her visitors. Helena was forced to blink to absorb the scene before her. Steel and glass furniture glinted in the sunlight that streamed through the picture windows. The floors were covered in pristine white carpets on which stood softly-padded couches. Mirrors reflected crystal vases, filled with an abundance of yellow roses, arranged throughout the apartment.

Gloria was resplendent in a dazzling yellow trouser-suit that picked up the colour of the roses, and her mane of dark hair fell softly to her shoulders. She displayed her dimples in a broad smile as she threw her arms around Max and Helena. Yetta cried tears of joy as she held her son and daughter-in-law close.

A dinner was arranged for that evening. All the members of the Harris family had been invited to meet Helena. Samuel's brother Isaac and his wife Lilian, with their sons Albie and Martin, were there too. The years had taken their toll on both Isaac and Lilian but the spark of humour and the warmth that had defined their contented union were still evident. Helena basked in the mellowness of the atmosphere.

Charlie Miller, who had sold his furniture store to the Harris brothers so long ago due to his arthritis, was also there in his wheelchair, with his wife Sarah who had withered with age and needed assistance to move about. Their elder daughter Dee had eventually married her university professor, Mark Stone, and they arrived from Cambridge where they had relocated after their marriage.

This would be only the first of many unforgettable family reunion dinners.

Helena marvelled at how smoothly Max reverted to the opulent lifestyle of his youth. Her heart surged with love when it became clear to her the extent of the luxurious lifestyle he had forfeited to travel to Israel. How easily he had adjusted to rural life on the kibbutz and to suburbia in Jerusalem.

It was a blisteringly hot day towards the end of their stay in New York. Helena stood before the open window of the apartment, a breeze teasing the curtains as she observed the bustle of the streets of New York far below, shimmering in the heat.

She became still, her thoughts reeling back to the innocence and security of her childhood with her family on Polna Street in Poland before the war. She remembered another hot morning when she and Sofia had walked out of the gates of Bergen-Belsen, pitifully thin, orphaned and stateless, and began their journey to freedom. How could she have envisaged that such an uncertain journey would, with time, lead her to this splendid apartment and into the warm embrace of another loving family? How blessed she felt.

Max walked into the room behind her, breaking into her thoughts. He held a glass of orange juice in his outstretched hand, the ice cubes rattling against the frosted glass.

"Why are you so quiet, Helena? What are you thinking?" he asked, handing the glass to her. "There is such a faraway look in your eyes."

She rolled the cool glass between her palms before sipping the liquid that slipped smoothly down her throat. Then she set the glass down and turned to Max, smiling radiantly. "I think it is time for us to go back to our home in Jerusalem and to Rachel and the twins," she answered. Nodding his agreement, Max wrapped her in his arms.

There would be many more visits that would include Rachel, Orit and Ilan. They too would become bonded with this warm and vibrant family.

Chapter 31

The photograph of Max in its simple wooden frame is placed next to their wedding photograph. Her eyes mist as she studies it. She feels the presence of Max. *Those no longer living*, she thinks, *are always with us*. Tenderly she caresses the image of Max with her fingertips, outlining his strong jaw and aquiline nose. His sweeping dark lashes fringe his soft brown eyes flecked with gold, as he gazes directly into the lens of the camera. It feels to Helena that time is obliterated.

Max had become a successful human rights lawyer and activist, taking up causes for Israelis and Palestinians alike. Disillusioned with the political situation in the Middle East, he worked tirelessly to help bring peace to the war-torn region.

Amir Dijani was a Palestinian lawyer who shared Max's ideology. He lived with his wife Uma and family in the suburb of Haifa. A chance meeting had brought the two lawyers together, leading to a lifelong friendship. Helena remembers the night Max arrived home much later than usual, his words tripping over each other as he described his encounter with Amir.

She smiles whimsically as the memory flutters behind her eyes and a soft nostalgia settles about her.

Max had been spending the day in court when his attention was drawn to a young Palestinian lawyer fiercely fighting his client's case. He admired the lawyer's eloquence and tenacity, and applauded when the verdict was delivered and the case was won.

Relaxing with the newspaper and a drink in the lawyers' canteen at the end of the day, Max noticed the same lawyer engrossed in his files at a nearby table. He strode over.

"Hello," he ventured. "I wish to congratulate you on winning your case today. It was a well-deserved victory."

A smile lit up the face of the young lawyer.

"Please join me," he replied, standing and gesturing for Max to take a seat. "I am Amir Dijani."

"Max Harris," said Max, extending his hand. He sat down at the table.

Time passed undetected as they spoke animatedly, exploring their common interest in the affairs of the Middle East. Discreetly Max glanced at his wristwatch and realised how much time had elapsed. He jumped up abruptly to leave, but not before a further meeting between the two lawyers had been arranged.

The deep bond that developed between Max and Amir extended to their families. Uma, Amir's wife, was an accomplished pianist and piano teacher. She rekindled Helena's love of music and her childhood dream of becoming a concert pianist. Together, the two couples attended many orchestral concerts that were playing to packed houses under the baton of Leonard Bernstein. They joined the throng of enthusiastic music lovers who crowded the venues, pushing through the masses to take their seats. They were swept away by the sheer joy of the soaring music, its mystical quality further bonding their friendship.

It was a fiercely hot summer's day. Not a leaf stirred. Even the birds had ceased their twittering as they huddled together on shady branches against the encroaching heat. Helena had returned home from the school at which she taught, a refreshing shower uppermost on her mind. She found Max waiting for her on the front porch, his arms folded across his chest and an enigmatic smile on his face. She glanced up at him, and raised her shoulders questioningly. He turned around and beckoned her to follow him. Then Max flung the front door wide open, to reveal a baby grand piano in the centre of the living room.

Helena's eyes widened in disbelief and her jaw dropped as she emitted a long "oh-h-h ..." Tenderly she brushed her arm across the shiny wood of the piano. Sitting down on the seat placed in front of it, she lifted the keyboard cover to display the pristine black and white keys beneath.

In that splinter of time, images of Maestro Trotsky flashed before her, and she raised her wrists above the keyboard. Reminiscent tunes guided her fingers tentatively to the notes until she grew more confident and the music reached a crescendo. Only then was she unable to hold back a flood of tears.

Max, wiping at his own wet cheeks, stood beside her while phantom images of Mameh and Tateh swaying in unison, hovered in the lengthening shadows.

Chapter 32

ISRAEL, PALESTINE

Max's credentials allowed him to pass freely through the security border, so he was able to visit Amir's family. He was always warmly welcomed by Amir's friends too; he was widely respected for his activism in the cause of restoring peace.

It seemed the Middle East was once again on the brink of war. Political tensions were escalating on both sides. Amir's brother Khalil had been detained in an Israeli prison after being arrested by Israeli police when he arrived at the checkpoint after curfew. Amir had appealed to Max to help secure his release.

After successfully crossing the border, Max arrived at Khalil's home where Amir's relatives had gathered. It was a warm day, the heat rising from the parched earth. Uma, together with Sura, Khalil's wife, had prepared the lunch table outside under a shady awning. A feast of shawarma, kefta and tabouli had been laid out, but a veil of gloom hovered over the lunch party. Sura was tearful and implored Max to bring her husband home.

While they were sitting around the lunch table, Max became aware of a sudden movement. Turning around, he caught sight of Ali, Amir's teenage nephew and Khalil and Sura's son, running towards the border wall. He had a rock in his hand, aimed at the Israeli armed guard. In that same moment, Max saw a sniper holding a gun aimed at the boy. Instinctively he jumped up and ran in pursuit of Ali. He reached him and lunged forward. He pulled him to the ground, covering Ali's body with his own.

It was too late for Max. The bullet intended for Ali entered Max's body. Life drained out of him, staining the dusty soil on which he lay a deep, dark, spreading red. And so Max Harris, beloved husband, father, human rights activist – a hero, breathed his last breath on the arid and unyielding soil of Palestine.

The events of that day remained sharply etched in Helena's memory.

It had been a challenging day in the classroom, with her young learners restless and distracted from their lessons. Then the bus ride home seemed interminable. She yearned to share the day's events with Rachel over a pot of freshly-brewed tea, and later that evening with Max when he returned from his visit with the Dijanis across the border. A cloud of concern for Max had hovered about Helena all day. She was aware that the situation in the territory was explosive, and that it could erupt into war at any moment; she would wait anxiously for his return.

That morning another letter had arrived from Ilan and Debra in America. With Rachel, and later with Max when he returned, Helena would pore over the eagerly-anticipated letter, absorbing every word. It brought them comfort to know that the young couple were adapting to life in a new country.

Arriving home, she was greeted by the tempting smell of freshly-baked pita bread. She kicked off her pumps and padded barefoot towards the kitchen from where the smell emanated.

Rachel stood before the stove stirring a pot of lentils. Helena stooped to kiss the top of her head before easing herself into a chair at the kitchen table. She breathed a long, drawn-out sigh of contentment.

"You look tired, *Schatzi*. Let me get you a cup of sweet, strong tea." Rachel moved towards the kettle. At the same moment that she lifted the kettle, there was an urgent hammering at the front door. With the kettle still in her hand, Rachel turned to Helena, her eyebrows raised questioningly.

Helena shrugged her shoulders and heaved herself out of her seat. "I'll go and see who is there."

Amir stood on the doorstep. He spoke just one word: "Max." His glazed eyes and wooden expression conveyed his dreadful message to her.

"Where is Max?" her voice trailed off and her breath caught painfully in her throat. Amir's face collapsed as he slumped towards her. And then Helena knew. She knew that her beloved Max was no longer alive.

Forever, she would remember that it was she, Helena, who cradled Amir in her arms comforting him. She felt as though she had been turned to stone.

It would be many days before she would know the relief that tears would bring. In the dark time that followed, it was only Rachel's gentle coaxing to eat and her children's support that penetrated her stupor. Shocked and grief-stricken, Ilan and Debra had returned to Israel and to the solace of Rachel's arms.

Helena appeared withered, her eyes lustreless. She was enclosed in an aura of solitude. Nothing anyone could say could lighten the unbearable grief thrust upon her.

A heartbroken Gloria and her husband Robert flew in from New York for the funeral and the week of mourning that followed. Gloria felt a deep affection for Helena and connecting with this strong woman whom her brother had loved so deeply brought her a measure of comfort. There was, however, no compensation for her loss of Max and it tore at her heart. She would simply have to endure the constant throb of pain that it brought.

For the past few years Yetta, her age well advanced, had been living in a care home where she dwelt in her own twilight world lost in the labyrinth of her mind. It was her Samuel's hand that held hers, not that of the kind nurse, and it was Samuel who fed her and hugged her, not Gloria, and so she spoke to him, her memory reaching deep into the past.

"Wait for me in America, Sam. How I shall miss you when you leave me, but I will come to you and bring Mamma's silver candlesticks with me. I will follow you to the end of the earth."

Soon, soon it would be Samuel who would take her hand and whisper to her: "Come with me, my love," and she would place each of her hands in each of his and, hand in hand and face to face, a sudden gust of wind would lift them into the air as she followed her Samuel to the end of the earth.

The rabbi paid Helena a visit after the week of mourning had been completed. She turned to him with downcast eyes. "I have lost so much," she said. "Now I have no more belief to cling to and I question the existence of a loving God."

The rabbi shook his head vehemently. "No, my child," he answered. "The hardest of life's lessons is to accept that over which we have no control, and to trust in the way of the Lord. It is not for us to question, but if you love and are loved in return, that person never leaves you and you never have to say goodbye. For now, you are needed by your family. I passed by your classroom on my way here today and your students eagerly await your return."

Helena looked up into the rabbi's eyes, and then the tears came.

The following morning, she was preparing to return to the classroom when the squeal of a bicycle's tyres outside the window drew her attention. Parting the curtains, she peered through the pane. Rachel was in the front garden conversing with a post office official who was standing next to his bicycle. She had been baking and her hands and arms were covered in flour. The postman held a bright gold-coloured telegram out to Rachel, and Helena watched Rachel signal to him to wait while she went back inside the cottage. She returned with a slice of warm apple strudel, which she handed to him before accepting the telegram. The young man thanked her, and pushing his postbag around to his back, he cycled away with a happy grin.

"*Schatzi*," Rachel called to Helena through the open doorway. "We have a telegram from Paris." By the time Helena reached her, Rachel had slit open the envelope and was dusting the flour off her hands. She flattened the telegram against her apron.

Leaning over Rachel's shoulder, Helena read the message:

Pierre has sold Pompadour and we are relocating to Jerusalem once arrangements are finalised. Soon we will be together again. Edie.

Rachel gave a whoop of joy, throwing her arms around Helena and leaving flour marks on her clothing. Laughingly, Helena dusted herself off. No one would ever replace Max but the devoted friendship of Edie and Pierre would help her face a future without him.

Chapter 33

The smallest of the photographs, in a gold frame, is placed slightly to the left of Max's photograph. In it, Ali Dijani, the boy whose life Max saved by sacrificing his own, stands tall and proud. He holds up a large silver trophy on which the bold lettered inscription of Max's name has remained clearly visible.

Helena takes a deep inward breath. Lifting the photograph, she lowers her head to study it.

Pain mingled with pride twists inside her like twin snakes.

Ali is now a grown man with his own family, but still there is an immutable bond between them.

Her gaze moves from the photograph and lingers on the mantlepiece where the trophy now stands, slightly apart from the silver candlesticks, and she is immersed in an unfolding memory.

The afternoon air was crisp and the trees were beginning to lose their crimson leaves, the warm autumn sounds dropping softly about. The tiny figure in the distance, trudging up the hill, was that of Rachel. As she crested the hill, a car drew up alongside her. It honked loudly, startling her. Uma leant out of the driver's-side window and beckoned to her.

"Rachel," she exclaimed. "That load in your shopping basket looks much too heavy. Hop in and I will give you a lift home."

Gratefully, Rachel sank onto the seat beside Uma and rubbed her calves.

"These legs are not as energetic as they used to be," she groaned. "But Uma, what are you doing here so far from home?"

"I have come to prepare my music students for a piano recital competition being held in Jerusalem tomorrow evening," Uma replied.

As they approached the house, Rachel turned to her. "I baked a batch of cinnamon buns this morning. Join Helena and me for tea. She is marking her students' reports and will be delighted to see you."

"You bake the best cinnamon buns."

Uma gave her a quick hug then climbed out of the car and retrieved Rachel's basket, which she carried into the house. Helena's face lit up when she saw them both. She and Uma embraced, exchanging pleasantries while Rachel got the kettle singing on the stove and laid out a tray of cinnamon buns dripping with melted butter.

While they were having tea, Uma's forehead puckered in thought. "I have enrolled my best music students in a competition tomorrow night. Please come along as my guests," she asked eagerly. "You will be pleasantly surprised at the high standard of music that these students are capable of producing."

She smiled happily when both women nodded their acceptance.

The concert hall was packed. A current of excitement ran through the audience. Helena and Rachel were seated close to the front of the stage, the first few rows being occupied by the contestants and their parents. Ali Dijani was among the contestants. He was now a head taller than his father Khalil, who sat beside him. They both turned to greet Helena when she entered the auditorium. She smiled back at them. But seeing Ali brought the cold reminder of all she had lost, and she attempted to swallow down the bitter taste that rose in her throat.

The contestants played faultlessly and Rachel and Helena joined in the enthusiastic applause at the end of each recital. Then it was time to announce the winner. When the judge stepped onto the stage there was a palpable air of anticipation as he held up a silver trophy. A hush fell over the expectant audience.

In a loud and gravelly voice, he said, "The winner of tonight's competition is ..." then, after a dramatic pause, "... Ali Dijani."

The audience exploded in applause as Ali walked up to the stage to accept the hard-earned trophy. He was about to return to his seat and to his proud parents, Khalil and Sura, when he hesitated, turned, and walked back to the middle of the stage. He searched the audience for Helena and locked eyes with her.

In a voice faltering with emotion, he said, "I am honoured to receive this prize, but there is something I need to say. I wish to dedicate this trophy to my hero, Max Harris, the man who sacrificed his own life to save mine."

He stepped to the front of the stage and spoke urgently and directly to Helena.

"I do not wish Max's death to be in vain. I shall forever carry the burden of his death, but what happened that day has taught me that hatred and aggression will only breed heartache and grief. I have witnessed the destruction and misery that one small stone can cause. Therefore, I have dedicated my life to continuing Max's ideology and I have formed a group of young people of all nationalities to perpetuate his cause. We call ourselves 'Seeds of Peace' and we strive for a better understanding among all the young people of this region."

He held the trophy towards Helena.

To a standing ovation, Helena was guided onto the stage. When the clapping subsided, she stepped up to Ali to receive the trophy.

Then, in a clear and modulated voice she said, "It was my husband's last wish that your life should be spared. The fine and talented young man that you have grown to be brings me immense comfort. Max's wish has been fulfilled, and I know that his memory will live on through your work to bring about justice and peace."

Gently, the vision fades away, surrendering her to the present, and she returns her attention to the photograph of Ali. For just a moment she lowers her lids thoughtfully and smiles to herself at Ali's youthful earnestness.

Once more, her gaze sweeps across the photographs positioned around her desk, settling on one that is partially concealed behind that of the twins. She feels a moment of joy as she pulls it towards her. Time has a way of diluting memories, but her visit with Ruth and Jonathan in South Africa remains sharply etched in her memory. Her eyes linger on the black and white photograph. The image of the three of them leaning against Jonathan's dusty Chevrolet, their heads thrown back in laughter, echoes the elation of that moment.

Helena places her elbows on the desk and nestles her chin in her upturned palms. A dreamy expression crosses her face as she allows her mind to drift back in time to the day fate made possible that which had seemed impossible.

Chapter 34

ISRAEL

The days following Max's death were dark as Helena navigated her way through despair and loneliness. A dense vacuum of grief enclosed her. Despite the care she received from those around her, this was one battle she had to fight alone.

And then came the telephone call from South Africa. Rachel was the first to reach for the phone.

"*Schatzi*, it's Ruth," Rachel called out, cradling the receiver with her hand beneath her chin and gesturing frantically with her other arm for Helena to take it from her.

A floodgate of emotion opened when Helena heard Ruth's voice. Stored-up grief poured out from the depths of her soul. Rachel stood silently by, waiting to comfort Helena as Ruth spoke soothingly to her.

"Lenie, Jonathan and I would like you to come to South Africa for a visit to our home in Paarl. It would be such a pleasure for us to be together again after all the years we have spent apart. The peace of the countryside will help you to heal. Please say that you will come," Ruth implored.

Helena's eyes widened. How could such an undertaking be possible? But Ruth was insistent.

"It is going to be my birthday. As a gift for both of us,

Jonathan is going to purchase a cruise line ticket for you to come to South Africa and spend some time with us."

"Give me a while to think it over ..." Helena ventured, overwhelmed at Ruth's proposal.

Rachel, overhearing the conversation, urged her to accept the offer. Within days, with Rachel's and Ruth's coaxing, she was drawn into the excitement of preparing for a visit to the Meyers' home in Paarl, South Africa. Hastily she applied for leave from the school at which she taught. It was readily granted by the sympathetic headmistress, Esther Burger. She had followed Helena's career closely and was struck by the rapport she had with the children. Esther felt that a holiday, away from the school for a while, would provide Helena with a chance to heal and to begin to come to terms with the tragedy of Max's death.

Two weeks later, on a drizzly February morning, Helena set sail aboard a cruise ship from Haifa, bound for Cape Town. Rachel had accompanied her in the taxi to the port, issuing instructions along the way to take care of herself. She had purchased a menorah set with precious Israeli stones as a gift for the Meyers and had wrapped it meticulously; it was included in Helena's luggage.

When they reached the docks, she embraced Helena, holding her close before she boarded the ship.

"Stay safe, *Schatzi*. I will see you in the light of the Sabbath candles until you return." She took Helena's face in both her hands and, standing on her toes, Rachel placed her lips tenderly against her friend's forehead.

Rachel had asked Marvin, the taxi driver, to wait for her until Helena boarded the ship. She climbed back into the taxi for the long drive back to Jerusalem. Loneliness engulfed her. Marvin attempted to make light conversation. Rachel answered him politely until he stopped trying and instead turned up the volume of the music on the car's radio.

In the stillness of her thoughts Rachel acknowledged that Helena had come to mean so much to her that being separated, even for a short while, left her feeling hollow and forlorn. She marvelled at how Helena, Max and the twins had filled the void left by the loss of her family, a loss for which she would forever bear the scars. Until she met Helena in the American Zone, her life had been only an existence. Now all that had changed.

Rachel rested her head against the back of the seat and let herself drift in a pool of remembrance. The music coming from the radio provided a soundtrack to her reflections of her life in Berlin before the war.

As a young girl growing up in Berlin, she had a glorious, golden future. Her family was part of a large Jewish community and was proudly German. Her paternal grandfather was a rabbi who served at one of the many splendid synagogues that were dotted throughout the city; the one in which Rachel would be married. The community thrived. Scientists, artists and doctors were among the members of the congregation who contributed to German academia.

Rachel was the middle sibling between her two brothers, both of whom performed in the Berlin orchestra. Her husband, Dieter, was the headmaster of a prestigious secondary school for boys. With the birth of their precious sons, Rachel felt that her life was complete.

Then the rumblings started. "Go," the people said. "Get out now before it is too late. Hitler cannot be trusted," they said. But the wise old men rocking back and forth around tables in the synagogues, stroking their beards, and the vivacious young mothers pushing strollers in immaculate, flowering parks, shook their heads. "We are German and we are respected by our neighbours. We are staying," they answered with one voice.

And then came Kristallnacht. It was a deep and abiding pain for Rachel when she suffered flashbacks of the scenes that came after ... streets littered with broken glass, the wailing, the screaming ...

By then it was too late.

Marvin's voice broke into her musings. "You are home, Madam," he said, opening the car door for her to step out.

Rachel entered the silent house. Straightening her shoulders, she felt a smile kindling inside her, sending its warmth into all the chambers of her heart. Helena would soon return and Orit and Raquel were sure to fuss over her until then.

She felt cherished.

Chapter 35

SOUTH AFRICA
1981

The ship docked in Cape Town harbour to a spectacular welcome. Cape Town had donned its finest attire to welcome its visitors. Helena stood on the deck, leaning against the railing. She was awed at the sight of the majestic Table Mountain that rose above the city. The solid blue sky was awash with the rays of the early morning sun glinting across the sea. They sparkled like diamonds on the crest of the gentle waves that lapped against the hull of the ship. The smell of salty sea air and fresh fish assailed her senses. Nothing could have prepared her for the kaleidoscope of sun, sea and sky that was Cape Town.

She lifted her face to the sun, feeling the warmth of Max's presence. "You are always beside me, Max. I draw on your strength. It is your love that sustains me," she whispered to the quiet of the morning. Time seemed to dissolve in the constancy of the expansive sky.

On the dockside, buskers and hawkers created a festive palette of vibrant colour. The air throbbed with their voices calling out to each other. Wares were being sold and assistance offered to the disembarking passengers.

Ruth and Jonathan were waiting expectantly for Helena on

the dockside. They pushed their way through the milling throng when they spotted her. Jonathan lifted Helena off her feet and whirled her around, to the amusement of the onlookers. There was Ruth, standing before her, the girl who had slithered down the orange tree to land at her feet and whose friendship had grown stronger through time and distance. Ruth's dark cropped hair was shot with silver and her olive skin weathered by an unrelenting African sun. The years had taken their toll, but her radiant smile remained unchanged, lighting up her face with the joy of being reunited with Helena.

The luggage was retrieved and together they bundled into Jonathan's open-top Chevrolet for the hour-long journey to Paarl.

The scenery changed, becoming more tranquil as they left the city and travelled through the countryside. The molten heat of summer intensified as they arrived in Paarl. Helena was struck by the sight of the large rock atop a low mountain range.

"That's Paarl Rock." Jonathan crouched over the steering wheel to point to it. "It was named by a Dutch settler because it resembled a pearl, 'Paarl' being the Dutch name for pearl. It had shimmered like a pearl in the morning dew" he explained. He cast a sideways glance at Ruth and added teasingly: "But Ruth is my pearl and the rock on which I lean."

Ruth and Jonathan had faced and overcome the disappointment of being childless, the pain thereof had drawn them even closer. Helena noted the deep affection that flowed between them and she revelled in its warmth. It evoked the memory of Max. His absence was a constant throbbing pain and left an emptiness that she felt could never be filled.

The serenity of Paarl was all-encompassing. The vineyards

stretched to the base of the mountain ranges that surrounded the town and formed a valley. Massive, ancient oak trees provided welcoming shade from the pulsating heat.

The Meyers lived in the Cape Dutch house once owned by Ruth's parents. It was still attached to the grocery store. Fronting the house was a wide porch, covered by a slanting asbestos roof painted green. Latticed cornices resembling lace adorned the edges of the sturdy pillars that held up the roof. Oak trees on the pavement offered relief from the heat.

Ruth showed Helena to a large, airy bedroom inside the house. A brass bed covered with a patchwork quilt took up most of the space and an overhead fan noisily churned up the hot air. But it was not yet time for bed and there was much to discover in this picturesque town.

In the mornings breakfast was served in the shade of the porch. Their neighbours, Ben and Elsa Strydom, joined them on most mornings. Elsa, renowned for her baking, usually provided a batch of freshly-baked butter rusks. She demonstrated to Helena how to dunk the rusks into the strongly brewed coffee before savouring them. As the flavours burst across her taste buds, Helena was jolted back in time to childhood days spent in the kitchen with Cook Berta as she prepared the meals, giving Helena spoonsful to taste. These different aromas took her back to the smells and tastes of her youth.

How she now appreciated the abundance of food spread before her. Remnants of memories when a stale crust of bread and a tin cup of thin soup would be her only meal for the day caused her to become contemplative. She recalled the days before liberation when her only sustenance was snow. She was engulfed in a wave of gratitude for the certainty that she would never again feel the pain of gnawing hunger that had consumed her in the camps.

Ben, a lawyer, and Elsa were a popular couple who had carved out a niche for themselves in the town. Ben was a giant of a man. His broad shoulders were emphasised by the brightly-checked shirts he wore and his height accentuated by the Stetson hat pushed back on his head. The moniker 'Big Ben' suited him well. His diminutive, shy wife Elsa contrasted sharply with his expansive demeanour and easily recognisable booming laugh that was often heard. The couple fascinated Helena and she was drawn to their warmth.

Minnie was the Meyers' housemaid. She was accommodated in a room in their back garden, and every morning she appeared in the kitchen to begin her daily tasks of cleaning and cooking. Her nut-brown skin was in sharp contrast to her crisp white apron. The floral headscarf wound around her head emphasised her broad gap-toothed smile and perceptive eyes in whose depths were reflected an ancient wisdom.

Since arriving in South Africa, Helena had been struck by the sight of the ebony- and lighter- brown-skinned people who were employed in menial labour. The sight of bare-chested men toiling in the heat at the roadside invoked memories. Visions flashed before her of the ghetto and the camps when Jewish men and women performed similar tasks, but without food or pay.

Ruth had encouraged Helena to visit the museum in the centre of Paarl. It was situated close to a church, and the clock at the top of the high steeple chimed every quarter of an hour, making it easy to locate. It was too hot to walk there, so Helena stood waiting patiently at the bus stop. She refused to sit on the bench on the pavement which had a plaque attached to it. Large white lettering on a black background declared: *WHITES ONLY*.

Soon a bus trundled up. Uncertain of the cost of the ride, Helena held out her palm filled with silver coins towards the conductor. He smiled, selected a few, and closed her hand around those remaining.

Helena settled onto a seat near the front of the bus, enjoying the scenery and the perfect summer day. At the next stop a black, elderly woman carrying a large parcel on her head boarded the bus. Helena's pulse quickened when she saw the woman being herded to the back of the bus although seats in the front were empty. A feeling of dread enveloped her. She remembered the laws that were passed in the early days of the war, laws that had delivered similar persecution to her family and all the Jews of Poland.

Helena was beginning to feel increasingly disturbed; a feeling that was difficult to suppress. She concluded that South Africa, with its pristine white beaches on whose powdery sands waves crashed and foamed, its undulating mountain ranges and cloudless blue skies created an impression of idyllic serenity. But it was a deceptive façade. Beneath its seductive beauty lay a dark and sinister undercurrent.

It was a particularly busy day in the grocery store and Ruth and Jonathan were attending to the long queue of customers, leaving Helena alone in the house. She was enjoying the still, cool morning when Minnie approached her.

"Does Missus want another cup of coffee?" she asked in broken English. She smiled at Helena, displaying the space that had once been occupied by her front teeth.

"Thank you, Minnie," Helena replied, smiling in return. "I will enjoy having coffee with you in the kitchen."

The aroma of coffee bubbling in the percolator on the gas stove greeted her, and Helena poured a mug full of the rich brew and settled herself at the kitchen table.

Leaning forward she gazed questioningly at Minnie. "Please tell me about yourself, Minnie, and about your family."

Minnie filled her mug with coffee and Helena pulled a chair away from the table, gesturing for Minnie to join her. She sat across from Helena, blowing at the steam rising from the cup resting between her upturned palms. Minnie's eyes appeared shadowed, and her slumped shoulders gave her a defeated look.

"Ai Missus, it is a hard life for us coloured folk. My family lives at the far end of town, over the bridge that crosses the Berg river. Most of the coloured people live there. Money is scarce, but we take whatever job comes our way so that we can earn a bit extra."

Helena's mind raced with questions. "Where did you go to school?" she asked.

"Oh Missus, I only went to school until I was twelve years old."

Helena lifted a hand to interrupt her. "Please don't call me Missus, Minnie. My name is Helena. But why did you leave school at such a young age?"

Minnie paused, her eyes submissively downcast. She fidgeted with the edge of her apron before replying. "My father worked hard to support our family and to pay the rent for the house we lived in. It was not much, but still my father struggled to come up with the money at the end of each month. Our landlord was sympathetic and made an offer to my father. If one of my father's daughters would become a nanny to his children, in exchange our family could live in the house rent-free. I was chosen.

"I left school and my family to live in a big house at the foot of the mountain to take care of the children. The family treated me well and I stayed with them for a few years, only coming home to my family one weekend a month. Then I was accused of stealing a hairbrush and sent home permanently in disgrace. It was too late to go back to school, therefore my parents sent me out to do domestic work. I am grateful to the Meyers. Not all domestic workers are treated as well as I am."

Minnie stood up from the table to collect the empty mugs. Standing with her back to Helena she rinsed the cups in the basin while continuing her monologue. "My mother worked in a fruit canning factory. The hours were long and the pay little, but there were good people who fought against the government to form unions. They worked actively to create better working conditions for the factory workers. Now my mother is too frail to work in a factory, but she still takes in washing and mending from the white folk."

Helena was pensive, quietly absorbing Minnie's story, when a tortured memory that had become blurred in the horrors of the past flashed before her.

"Minnie," she said, addressing her back. "I too have a story to tell you. Please, sit down again."

Minnie wiped her wet hands against her apron and joined Helena at the table. She placed an elbow on the table and, cupping her cheek in her hand, she gazed questioningly at her.

"I was once a housemaid," said Helena softly, returning Minnie's gaze.

"How can that be?" Minnie shook her head in wide-eyed disbelief.

Helena leant towards Minnie, stretching her arms across the table. Caught in a sliver of time, her memory became sharper and her story unfolded.

The *Aufseherin*, or overseer, of Auschwitz had selected Helena from among the women of the camp to clean her home and perform all the duties of a housemaid. Her fair colouring had led the overseer to mistake Helena for a *Mischling*, a child of mixed Jewish and German race; besides, she was beautiful and did not resemble the grotesque caricatures of Jewish people displayed on posters throughout the cities. So, the *Aufseherin* deemed her suitable to clean her house.

Each morning Helena set off to the overseer's house beyond the confines of the camp. How easily she could run away, she thought. But there was nowhere to hide and in her striped pyjamas and shaven head, she would be clearly visible. The food she was given at the overseer's home encouraged her to return daily so that she could take food back with her to share with the women inmates at the camp.

Helena, who had had a cossetted childhood filled with the love and care of her family as well as that of nannies and teachers, was made to scrub floors and wash bundles of clothes under the merciless eye of the *Aufseherin* until her scraped knees bled and the skin on her red and calloused hands peeled.

The food she received was compensation for the hardship she endured, but this too came to an end when she, along with other inmates of Auschwitz, was moved to another camp. However, it was the food given to her by the overseer, which she had been able to share, that played a significant role in her survival.

The Death March towards Bergen-Belsen was hazardous. Many of the inmates died from cold and hunger, and bodies frozen in ice were strewn along the way. Any prisoner who stumbled or fell was instantly shot by one of the Nazi soldiers that guarded the group.

The route took the desperate, barely-living inmates past homes wherein the occupants could be seen eating their meals and continuing with their tasks, while peering through the windows at the bedraggled prisoners. No heed was given to them, no compassion shown. They appeared oblivious to the suffering of these tortured men and women.

Helena had lost her shoes in the snow and every step she took sent a shard of unbearable pain shooting up her legs. She was tempted to remove the shoes from the corpses along the route but her respect for the dead prevented her from doing this. Wracked with cold and hunger, Helena stumbled. As she was about to fall, a woman prisoner appeared on either side of her, propping her up. The women supported her, part-dragging her along with them, until she was able to find her footing.

"You gave us the bread that you were given by the *Aufseherin*," one of them whispered to her. "Without it, we would have perished. Now it is our turn to save your life."

When the group eventually arrived at Bergen-Belsen, they were greeted by the unimaginable sight of dead bodies piled up as high as a mountain.

Minnie, transfixed by Helena's story, sat riveted, not uttering a sound until they heard Ruth arriving at the front door. Then, with a deep sigh, saddened by the tale that she had just heard, she pushed herself away from the table.

"Hullo-o. Anyone home?" Ruth sang out, entering the kitchen and ending Helena's conversation with Minnie. "Ben and Elsa have invited us for lunch today." She lowered herself into a chair beside Helena, who nodded eagerly at the news of the invitation. She had grown fond of the couple and enjoyed their company. They waited for Jonathan to return, and then the three of them set out for lunch.

They were welcomed by the Strydoms. Elsa had laid out the meal on a sturdy yellowwood table beneath the awning of the veranda that overlooked a rose garden. The open blooms created a carpet of colour, their delicate perfume filling the air. Bees seeking nectar buzzed lazily among the roses, their humming the sound of a whispered prayer. The tranquillity of the scene caused the vision of Max once again to appear before Helena, intensifying the ache in her heart.

Elsa had prepared a lavish feast for her guests. Bobotie, samoosas, saffron rice, lamb bredie and boerewors rolls were piled in dishes across the table. In the centre a bottle of wine from the vineyards of Paarl lay resting in a frosted holder.

The conversation around the table was light-hearted, but Helena was distracted by the story Minnie had told her and she found her mind wandering. Ben noticed how pensive she had become and turned to her. "You seem troubled, Helena," he said.

Meeting Ben's penetrating gaze Helena sighed deeply before speaking of the troubling observations she had made in South Africa, among them the bus trip she had undertaken. "How has this come about, Ben?" she asked. "Max was a lawyer and human rights activist ..." she paused for a moment, staring into the distance to consider Max's reaction. "He would have been as concerned as I am."

Ben pulled up his shoulders in a helpless gesture. "It is the law of the current government of this country. As a lawyer, I fight to overturn these laws and help those most affected. Fortunately, Nelson Mandela did not receive the death sentence and has been imprisoned on Robben Island instead. While we fight for his release and for democracy, I am afraid it is an uphill battle. But those of us who fight for this will never give up."

Ben's eyes lit up as a thought struck him. "Tomorrow I am defending a young man, Sipho Qobo. Why not come with me to the courthouse and witness the legal aspects of the case I am defending? I will arrange a seat for you in the courtroom."

Helena turned to Jonathan and Ruth, raising her eyebrows questioningly for their opinion.

"Go on, Helena," they chorused. "You will find it interesting."

Chapter 36

The following morning, Helena waited for Ben on the pavement beneath the shade of the trees. The dry oak leaves and acorns crunched and crackled beneath her sandals. The day felt fresh. She wore a white linen blouse with wide sleeves that reached to her elbows and a blue floral skirt. She had pinned back her hair in anticipation of the day's heat, and a straw hat with matching blue floral band framed her delicate features.

She didn't have to wait too long before Ben's burgundy and cream Vauxhall pulled up alongside. Ben, too, was suitably attired for court. The checked shirt and Stetson hat were replaced with a sombre-looking suit and tie, rendering him almost unrecognisable.

On the short trip to the courthouse, Ben familiarised Helena with Sipho Qobo and the matter that he would be defending on his behalf.

By South African law, all black people were forced to own and carry a passbook which enabled the authorities to monitor their movements and control their rights to work in a so-called 'white' area. It was considered a crime if the passbook could not be produced when requested by a law officer. Sipho worked for a supermarket, using his bicycle to deliver groceries to customers. He had been stopped by a policeman on his way home from work and asked to produce his passbook. A bolt of fear shot through him when he realised that it was not in his pocket and that he might have lost it during his deliveries. The unsympathetic policeman would have none of it and hauled Sipho off to a prison cell where he remained for days, waiting for his trial to come to court.

Ben had become aware of Sipho's predicament and, angered by the attitude of the policeman, he offered him pro bono assistance.

The courthouse with its pristine white walls surrounded by lush green lawns created a picturesque setting. It was bordered on one side by a girls' school and on the other by a park with a flower garden. The sound of gurgling water fountains mingled with the voices of children calling to each other.

Inside the austere courtroom, the atmosphere was gloomy. Helena took a seat on the wooden bench near the front. The bespectacled, white-haired judge appeared in his black robe, his face scrubbed to a pink sheen. Once the case proceeded, Sipho shuffled forward with his feet in shackles. Helena was mesmerised by his look of tired defeat and the sadness in his face.

Ben fought hard, using compelling arguments. His strong opinion reverberated throughout the courtroom. He was able to prove that a few days prior to the incident before the court, Sipho had produced his passbook when stopped by the same policeman. This proved beyond doubt that he had one and that it was conceivable that he had subsequently lost it. The judge grudgingly agreed with Ben and a verdict was passed. Sipho was sentenced to a fine of ten rand, or six months in prison if he could not come up with the money. Sipho did not have the required funds so Ben paid on his behalf, and he was now a free man.

The judge left the courtroom and Helena went up to where Ben and Sipho were filling out forms to complete his release and to apply for a new passbook. Helena took Sipho's hand to congratulate him. Tears of gratitude glistened in his soft brown eyes as he shook her hand and then Ben's, but he was anxious to return to his home.

The sadness that Helena had seen in Sipho's face would linger in her memory long after she had left South Africa to return to Israel. It was as though he had touched her soul.

But her time spent in Paarl also held many moments filled with spontaneous laughter. On the drive home from the courthouse, she observed Ben driving on the wrong side of the road on the back street leading to the Meyers' home.

"Why?" she asked.

"Well, you prefer the shady side, don't you?" was his laconic reply, followed by his booming laughter. Helena joined in, laughing so hard that she was left gasping for air and holding her sides.

It would come to pass that Helena would be in South Africa again, when the country became democratic. She would forever remember the sight of the long, snaking queues leading up to the voting booths and the feeling of euphoria that wrapped itself around the entire population.

For now, the long, hot, lazy days spent with Ruth and Jonathan were passing too quickly. Helena luxuriated in their camaraderie, and the care and kindness of their neighbours, who generously provided a continual feast of traditional South African dishes.

A plaited doughnut filled with a sweet syrup was Helena's favourite pastry; she was determined to take the recipe back to Rachel and so bring a small part of South Africa to Israel.

The African sun had replaced the pallor of Helena's cheeks with a healthy glow and the contented days had eased her pain as Ruth had predicted. She noted that Helena's eyes had lost their dullness and that the tears she had shed when first arriving in Paarl were now replaced with smiles when memories of Max surfaced.

The Meyers' home rang with peals of laughter when Helena and Ruth reminisced about the time that they had met in the orange grove, retelling how Ruth had slithered down the tree to land at Helena's feet. Jonathan got caught up in their infectious laughter, doubling up with mirth, his shoulders heaving as he spluttered and gulped to catch his breath.

It was the sound of the happiness of that laughter that would follow Helena back to Israel, to Rachel, her family and her homeland, and would remain branded in her memory as clearly as the prisoner number that was tattooed on the inside of her arm.

Sadly, Helena prepared to take leave of her friends and South Africa for the boat trip back to Israel, but not before she had extracted a promise from them to visit Israel the following year.

Chapter 37

ISRAEL

The months flew by, and the Meyers and Strydoms fulfilled their promise. They arrived at Ben Gurion airport on a stifling day in August when the air hung heavy with heat. Helena was there to greet them and to ease them through the congested airport. With their baggage retrieved, they were soon settled into a cab and on their way back to Jerusalem. The visitors were accustomed to the heat of Paarl but this dry, hot wind was different: it left their skins feeling gritty and their eyes dry. Laughingly, Helena assured them that there was a cool shower waiting for them and an airconditioned bedroom.

On the drive to Jerusalem, Ben hung out of the window exclaiming in wonderment at the bustling cities and towns through which they passed. He was astonished at the lush green foliage where only a few decades ago there had been arid desert.

Back at their home, Rachel was waiting for the arrival of the guests. She had spent days in the kitchen preparing meals for their impending visit. Now that she had mastered the art of making the perfect South African koeksister, the little plaited doughnuts were bubbling in a pot of syrup on the stove until they turned crisp and golden, their fragrance filling every room of the house.

Just days before, there had been an emotional reunion when Ilan, Debra and the children had arrived in Jerusalem from America. They were staying at a nearby hotel but spent their days with Rachel and Helena, and the house rang with laughter and happy reminiscences.

Soon it would be the memorial of Max's death, and a candle that would burn for twenty-four hours would be lit. It gave Helena a feeling of comfort to know that all her children would be with her to commemorate this day. Gilad, Sara and little Benjamin scampered about the garden eagerly awaiting the arrival of their aunts, Orit and Raquel, and cousin David who would be arriving the following day.

The previous year, Orit and Raquel had adopted David from a Palestinian orphanage. The energetic little boy with a mop of dark curls, huge brown eyes and an infectious smile completed their family and crept into the hearts of all who met him.

Helena and Rachel looked forward to the days that little David spent with them while Raquel and Orit worked long hours at the research laboratories. Then their home would be filled with bursts of laughter as Helena and Rachel chased after the active child. It seemed his energy never waned but towards evening he would creep into a lap of either Helena or Rachel. His eyes with their fringe of thick lashes would eventually droop and the two women would breathe a sigh of contentment as they watched over the sleeping child.

When Ilan was introduced to David he was captivated by the boy. He knelt down to meet David's eyes. "Hey there, little fella," he said, tousling his curls. David returned Ilan's smile, solemnly holding out a little hand. He chortled gleefully when Ilan swung him up onto his broad shoulders and cantered around the room with him, with all the children in tow.

The Dijani family, Amir, Uma and the children, arrived to join the celebratory lunch that Rachel had prepared. A trestle table had been set up in the garden beneath the shady trees. It seemed to groan under the weight of the platters filled with Israeli, Palestinian and South African dishes. At the heart of the jovial group, Helena and Rachel beamed happily. Max felt so close to them that it was as though they could invoke his spirit and visualise him beside them, sharing the pleasure of being among their loved ones.

Ben and Amir struck up an instant friendship, exploring the many interests they had in common. After the meal the two men spent the remainder of the day in deep conversation discussing the politics of the times. Amir was drawn to Ben, seeing in him the same characteristics that had defined Max.

With the passage of time, Ben would often return to Israel, renewing his friendship with Amir as crucial events in both countries unfolded.

The South African visitors were determined to make the best of their stay in Israel despite the fierce heat. They frolicked in the cool sea water of Eilat and shrieked with laughter when Ben floated in the Dead Sea, unable to regain his balance or stand upright. The view from the top of Masada left them breathless, and its fascinating history, incredulous. They listened in awe to the story of the Judeans under siege by the Romans. They were told that when it became evident that the Romans would take over Masada, all the Judeans, but for two women and five children who hid in the cisterns, took their own lives. These few survivors were able to pass the story on, into the annals of history.

The South Africans learned to push their way onto buses and *sheruts*, emulating the locals. They made their way through the *shucks* surprised at the vast array of merchandise on sale. They devoured the *shakshuka* breakfasts of eggs simmering on a bed of tomatoes and garlic and mopped up the dripping gravy with hot naan bread.

Crossing over the border into Jordan was a highlight of their stay. The lost city of Petra with its towering pillars and temples carved out of sandstone would forever be emblazoned on their memories.

In Haifa the visitors were welcomed by Raquel's parents who owned a restaurant, and they were treated to a lavish Palestinian meal. All afternoon they relaxed beneath the shade of the trees in the garden of the restaurant, sampling the continuous array of dishes being ferried to their table from the kitchen. They consumed golden dates, kebabs, hummus and knafeh with relish, and wiped plates of freekeh clean with pita breads. When the last golden rays of the setting sun had dipped over the horizon and the sky was splashed with stars, they reluctantly took leave of their hosts. They had bonded with their new friends and were determined to return to the restaurant before their visit to Israel ended.

Tel Aviv with its magical nightlife was a revelation. It appeared to them to be a city that never slept. In contrast they experienced a deep sense of peace when visiting the Wailing Wall – the Kotel – and shed tears when they viewed museums portraying the hardships experienced in the founding of the

Jewish state.

People of all nationalities and religions mingled happily in the labyrinths of the vibrant Old City, creating a rainbow of colour. The South Africans indulged in the many offerings of memorabilia on sale and returned with their arms laden with gifts to take back home with them.

All too soon it was time to leave Israel, and after an emotional farewell they boarded the plane bound for South Africa. As the plane left the runway, Ben, Elsa, Ruth and Jonathan turned to each other and unanimously agreed that they had each left a bit of their heart behind in Israel.

Chapter 38

ISRAEL

1990

Helena remembers the events of yesterday and is catapulted back into the present.

She is clearing out her desk for the very last time. A reluctant autumn sunrise is breaking through the clouds, sending shards of light to illuminate the dusty corners of the classroom. Many years of teaching are bound up in her memories and she is engulfed with nostalgia. She reads and rereads the notes and studies the drawings given to her by her young students throughout her teaching career. Some of those students are now parents themselves.

She has hoarded these notes and drawings, too precious to destroy, in the classroom cupboard. Now she places them in a cardboard box to be collected by the cleaners. *Time to let go.* She sighs deeply, thinking of the generations of children who have passed through her classroom leaving a lasting impression on her life as she has on theirs. She knows she will always be their beloved '*Morah* Lenie'. But her life is once again on the cusp of change. Besides, Rachel has become so frail. She has devoted her life to caring for Helena, Max and the twins; now it is she who needs to be cared for.

Helena is immersed in her thoughts when a shadow falls across her desk and a deep male voice with a distinct Polish accent enquires: "I am looking for Helena Jablonski. Can you help me?"

Surprised at hearing her maiden name, she looks up expectantly, answering in Polish. "Yes, I am Helena."

A broad smile breaks across the kindly face before her. "I am Igor Fisher, the son of Dr Anton Fisher. My father tended to Sofia before she died. I am delivering an envelope from her to you."

His words sends spasms of shock through Helena and she places her forearms on the desktop, dropping her head into her hands. Igor Fisher, a man of considerable size, lowers his bulky frame into a chair beside her. Sensing Helena's distress, he covers her hands with his large ones and begins his story.

As a teenager, he told her, he lived with his parents in the cottage next to Nadia's. He remembered the sorrow that afflicted his family when Sofia died. He remembered too that Nadia, soon after Sofia's burial, joined a group that managed to cross the border into Austria by travelling through the forest at night. Before Nadia left, she handed Dr Fisher an envelope containing a letter written by Sofia and addressed to Helena in Paris.

Shortly after Nadia left Poland, Anton Fisher suffered a stroke to which he succumbed, and Igor and his mother remained in the cottage until his mother's death. Igor married and brought his young wife to live in the cottage, where they raised their three sons.

A cellar underneath the house served as a storeroom. When Jacub, their youngest son, was preparing to leave for college, he rummaged through the boxes and discarded furniture in the cellar in search of a suitcase. When he came across his grandfather's medical bag, he opened it and found the envelope addressed to Helena nestling within the leather folds of the bag.

Jacub handed the letter to Igor, who was incredulous at its appearance after so much time had passed. He felt the weight of responsibility for delivering the letter to its intended recipient. He tried contacting Nadia, whom he hoped would shed some light on Helena's whereabouts, but all his attempts were in vain. There appeared to be no further record of Nadia once she had left Poland.

It would be many months later, long after he had given up hope, that he would receive an answer to his queries. It was contained in a letter from the administration office of a hospital in Vienna, informing him of Nadia's death some years previously. The administrator provided details relating to Nadia from the time of her arrival in Vienna.

The group led by Tomasz Nowak had safely crossed the border and entered a displaced persons' camp. Many of the residents were malnourished and sick, and the selfless Nadia assisted the mothers to care for their children.

Katy was a reed-thin Hungarian child who was six years old but could have passed for much younger. She was part of a large family living in the camp, all of whom required care, so when she took ill and was admitted to hospital Nadia offered her help. Katy's distraught mother gratefully accepted.

Nadia stayed at the hospital with little Katy. She slept besides Katy's bed at night and cradled her in her arms during the day. It was there, in Nadia's arms, that Katy gently breathed her last little rasping breath. Then Nadia fell ill and was diagnosed with the same disease that had consumed Katy. When she too faded gently away, her death certificate stated that she had died of tuberculosis. Those who were closest to Nadia, knew that she had died of a broken heart.

Igor was determined to deliver the letter and set out to find Helena Jablonski to whom it was addressed in Paris. He travelled to Paris and made his way to the Blums' apartment on the Rue des Rosiers. But Jacques and Amelie had moved to America and the new owners of their apartment had no further knowledge of them, nor of Helena.

Chapter 39

1950

PARIS - NEW YORK

When Jacques and Amelie arrived back in Paris after attending Max and Helena's wedding in Israel, their apartment felt emptier and lonelier than it ever had before. Spending time with Rachel and Helena had made them aware of how much they missed them both and how they longed to be part of a family again.

The silence in the apartment was oppressive, their voices echoing off the walls. Celeste and Violetta would be returning for their summer holiday, but that was still months away.

Spring had slipped between the days, bringing a feeling of renewal. The fiery shades of burnished copper, crimson and gold that once painted the landscape had long since faded into the grey of winter. Now, once again, the apple blossom tree was proudly displaying its tiny pink buds.

Jacques was reclining in his favourite chair in front of the hearth in the study as daylight faded into dusk. He was immersed in his thoughts, gazing at the crackling embers. Their glow illuminated his features tinged with worry and cast shadows against the wall.

The door of the study opened and Amelie entered quietly. Sinking into a chair beside him, she said, "You look troubled, *mon chéri.*" When he turned to face her, the purposeful look on his face told her all she needed to know. She leaned towards him, solemnly taking his hand in her own and returned his gaze.

"Jacques, it is time to move on," she said earnestly. "This apartment has become too big for us. Let us go to America, to our daughters, and be a complete family once again."

Jacques heaved a sigh of relief and his troubled expression was replaced with a smile.

"Now how could you have known what I was thinking?" he asked, the twinkle returning to his eyes.

"After so many years of marriage, I can read your thoughts." She replied laconically patting the top of his head.

Within weeks, a 'Sold' sign was prominently displayed across the front door of their apartment. They donated most of the contents, as well as the Renault, to Father Francis and Sister Madeleine's cloister as a token of their gratitude for the protection provided to their daughters throughout the war.

When the day came for them to leave, Father Francis insisted on driving them to the airport. Once again, the Blums piled into the Renault with the roof retracted, as it had been when they accompanied Rachel and Helena to the train station. Only this time, it was their own lives that were about to change.

The decision to join their daughters in New York turned out to be a sound one. Guided by Celeste and Violetta, they easily settled down to the American way of life. Soon they were lunching on bagels and lox, exclaiming over the view from the top of the Empire State Building and vigorously shouting encouragement to the players of the baseball team which they supported.

In December they displayed Chanukah lights together with Christmas trees in their apartment. While snowflakes drifted about them, they warmed their hands on the brown paper packets containing hot chestnuts, and even brought home more to roast. As the years passed, Celeste and Violetta married and had children of their own. Their visits to the Blums' apartment were always exuberant and provided Jacques and Amelie with the feeling of family connection that they had yearned for.

With the steady drip of time, Jacques and Amelie slipped contentedly into the evening of their lives.

Until tragedy struck.

Amelie was preparing breakfast for Jacques early one morning when she stumbled blindly against the kitchen table, calling out in pain. Jacques reached her just as she collapsed against him.

With sirens blaring, an ambulance transported Amelie to the same hospital where once Charlie Miller's brother Danny, now retired, had been the resident neurosurgeon. The doctor who examined Amelie was solemn as he conveyed the details of Amelie's condition to Jacques. She had suffered a stroke and her condition was inoperable. The prognosis was grave.

In the weeks that followed, Amelie lingered, drifting in and out of consciousness.

It was a midnight call that had alerted Helena and Rachel to the seriousness of Amelie's illness. Celeste had put the call through to Israel, miscalculating the time difference between the continents, and the jarring ring of the phone caused the two women to tumble from their beds, drowsy and confused. Helena was the first to reach for the receiver. Hearing the anguish in Celeste's voice dissolved her sleepiness and she drew Rachel close to include her in the conversation.

"My father, Jacques, is not coping well with my mother's illness and Violetta and I are concerned for his health," said Celeste, her voice echoing down the phone lines. The women, shocked at hearing Celeste's account of Amelie's condition, locked eyes and simultaneously mouthed: "Let's go."

"Celeste," Helena said before replacing the receiver, "Rachel and I will be with you as soon as we are able to book a flight to New York. You are not alone."

The sound of Celeste crying quietly at the other end, and her "thank you" in a voice strangled with emotion, confirmed to the two women that their decision was the right one.

Helena was startled at Jacques' stricken appearance as he sat beside his unconscious wife, his eyes never wavering from her. She observed how the years had taken their toll: his hands were gnarled and spotted with age, his eyes hooded and dull.

For Amelie, drifting in and out of consciousness, it was as though her life was written on the loose pages of a book that fluttered about her. It told the story of an urchin child in ragged clothing who danced for pennies in the backstreets of Paris ... until the pages settled gently around her and she peacefully descended into the shadows of her life.

After the funeral, Helena and Rachel prepared to leave the Blum family and head back to Israel and home. They grieved for Amelie who had been a beautiful and compassionate woman and who had so generously offered them comfort when they needed it most. Helena gulped back tears as she folded Jacques in her arms, alarmed at the boniness of his shoulders. A spasm of dread shot through her as she experienced a premonition that these would be their last moments together. Besides her cousins, Jacques was her only surviving family member. It was he who had offered her a home and helped her mend her broken life after the war when she had lost all that she treasured, and she loved him dearly.

Before she and Rachel left the Blum's and New York to return home, Helena placed her hands on either side of Jacques' weathered cheeks and tilted his face close to hers. She repeated the words that she had uttered to him so long ago in Paris:

"In your eyes I see my mother." Then she placed her own cheek, wet with tears, against his.

They both sensed that this would be their last goodbye.

Chapter 40

In Paris, when Igor Fisher was unable to uncover any information about the Blum family or Helena, he felt as though his search had come to an end. He was deflated but determined not to give up on his mission. After some thought, he decided that a visit to the City Archives might well yield information on Helena.

A fine drizzle misted the city as he set off on foot the following morning, the damp seeping through his clothing. He took many wrong turns before he finally located the archives in the late afternoon. The archivist manning the front desk was a stern-looking, thin-lipped French woman, her hair scraped back in a severe bun. She informed him that it was ten minutes to closing time and that he should return the following day.

Igor was determined to complete his mission and so he mustered all his charm. "Madame, I can see in your eyes that you are a good and kind woman. I have travelled all day to reach you and with your help I know I shall find what I search for," he pleaded, his eyes fixed on hers.

Her stern demeanour softened and with a terse smile she allowed him entry to the archives. Igor was left alone in the dimly-lit, musty-smelling room that lined with shelves containing cardboard files. Then the archivist reappeared, having warmed to Igor's appeal.

"Let me help you," she said, "before it gets too late and I will have to close the archive."

Igor ran his finger down the list headed 'J' in the file. It didn't take long to uncover information about Helena Jablonski, and now he had his first lead. Together he and the archivist replaced the files on the shelves and, with a show of gratitude, Igor kissed her hand before leaving. He had uncovered information revealing that Helena had been employed at a millinery factory called Pompadour, but the business had been sold and new owners were in charge.

Now that he had a trail to follow, he hurried back to the hotel he was staying at, only stopping along the way to buy a long, freshly-baked baguette and a slab of strong cheese for his dinner. Once in the hotel room, he undressed wearily and took a long, hot shower. Refreshed, and wrapped in a warm robe, he ate his dinner by lamplight at a small round table close to the window. He watched the raindrops splash down the pane, turning the lights of Paris into a prism of colour.

Before preparing for bed, he rummaged in his overnight bag and withdrew the letter that he had set out to deliver. Although weightless, in his hand it felt as heavy as a bar of gold. Carefully, he slipped it back into his bag and turned out the light.

The following day his search for the original owner, Pierre Lamont, and his wife Edie proved futile. The only information he could uncover was that after selling Pompadour many years ago, the Lamonts had left Paris to settle in Israel. Still not prepared to give up, Igor made his way to Pompadour. He hoped that there might be an employee who remembered Helena. He questioned each worker, but nobody had any recollection of her. It seemed he had once again drawn a blank.

Disheartened, he was about to leave when a toothless woman

with stringy grey hair tugged at his sleeve. She was bent over a broom with which she was sweeping the factory floor.

"I remember Helena," she said, with a raspy breath. "I was a child when my mother worked here. She often spoke of the splendid party that was held for Helena in the Lamonts' home before she left Paris to settle in Palestine."

Igor thanked her, pressing some silver into her palm. She beamed a gummy smile and bent her head to kiss his hand. At last Igor had the lead he was searching for and he hastily booked a flight headed for Israel.

Once there it was not difficult to find Helena through government inventories. Now here he was before her, handing her the envelope containing Sofia's letter.

Helena recognised the familiar handwriting on the envelope and was suffused with emotion. She sat perfectly still with her head bowed, absorbing Igor's story. She had so many questions to ask him and she wanted to find the words to convey her gratitude for the journey he had undertaken to deliver this precious envelope to her.

But when she looked up, he was gone. His mission was accomplished.

EPILOGUE

Chapter 41

ISRAEL

1990

The envelope lies on the desktop, beckoning, drawing her irresistibly towards it. Helena lifts it and breaks the seal. The contents spill out onto the desk, and she leans closer, her heart lurching as she recognises the sepia print portrait of her family. This is the only one she will ever have. Mesmerised, she lifts it to the light to study it.

In the portrait her mother is seated, her expression serene, her hands folded in her lap as she gazes, it seems to Helena, directly at her. She remembers the blue dress with the tucked bodice that her mother wore specifically for this occasion. Her father, the patriarch, stands behind her mother, his hands resting on her shoulders. His serious expression and thick eyebrows do not hide his twinkling eyes.

And there they are.

The two little girls, Eva and Helena, standing demurely on either side of their parents, their faces lifted up to the camera untouched by the future. They are dressed in matching white smock dresses with large bows pinned into their neatly-brushed curls. In this portrait of a perfect family, there is no hint of the devastation that would befall them.

Gazing at it, Helena feels that time has been breached and she is transported back to the moment that the picture was taken. She remembers the fussy photographer in his pinstriped waistcoat who kept disappearing under the large black hood of his tripod camera. He rearranged their positions until he was satisfied that the portrait would be perfect.

Tenderness softens Helena's features as she studies it intently. She turns the photograph over. There is a date on the back: 1937. Although the ink has begun to fade, it is still legible. Beneath it is an inscription in Sofia's neat handwriting:

Nadia retrieved this photograph from your home soon after you and your family had been sent to the ghetto. The apartment had been ransacked by the Nazis. Only this photograph was discarded, and she found it lying on the bare wooden floor.

A cream-coloured sheet of writing paper lies folded beside the photograph. Gingerly Helena unfolds it. She becomes aware of the slowing of her breath as she begins to read.

Dearest Helena,

Now I know that we shall not meet in Palestine. However, if this should reach you when you are there, our promise to each other will be fulfilled. You, who have survived, are to bear witness for those of us who have not. This is your privilege, as life is your gift. Now that I am so ill, I wish to remember only the best times of my life. Nadia reads to me and reminds me of the blissful times we shared as children on Polna Street. I have grown to love Nadia, who cares for me so diligently, as I have loved you. Do not mourn me but celebrate my life with

yours. Your children and grandchildren will be consecrated to the future of our people. Remember me, for my soul will be in the spiritual light of your Sabbath candles.
My dearest Lenie, remember me.
Sofia

Helena reads and rereads the letter. She hears Sofia's voice reverberate in the empty space, her words falling softly like petals about her. "I love you," Helena whispers into the surrounding silence. Her hands tremble slightly as she places the contents back into the envelope. Images from the past remind her of all she has lost.

"*And yet,*" she thinks, "*I have loved and have been loved in return. And still I have so much more love to give.*"

A movement behind her intrudes into her thoughts, spiralling her back into the moment. Rachel has woken from her nap and stands behind her chair. She places her hands on Helena's shoulders and stoops to rest her cheek against Helena's.

"*Schatzi,*" she says, her voice still throaty with sleep. "It's sundown and time to light the Sabbath candles."

The candlelight bathes the room in a soft amber glow. Serenely, Helena and Rachel stand side by side in front of the candles as the flames burn brightly.

Helena covers her eyes with her palms in prayer, perfectly at peace.

Acknowledgements

This book may never have seen the light of day had it not been for Jennigay Coetzer and the members of the Writers Friendship Group. I am grateful to each one of you for your encouragement, support and critical input. You believed in me long before I believed in myself. Thank you for coming on this journey with me.

A huge thank you to my talented and dedicated team, Tertius Van Eeden, publisher, Fiona Rom and Lorem Ipsum (Pty) Ltd, editors, and Ruan Wiggett, technological go-to-girl. It is your professionalism that I admire and your friendship that I value.

Friends, and strangers that became friends, took time out to read my first draft and cheered me on. There are too many to mention but I am eternally grateful to each and every one of you. A special thank you to Gwynne Robins, Tanya Barben, Leonard Suransky, Linda Orlando and Beryl Eichenberger.

Amanda, Tamara and Pablo, you are, undoubtedly, the wind beneath my wings.

I am fortunate to have a marriage partner who has always given me the space to dream and the courage to make my dreams come true. Thank you, Henry, love you forever.

In loving memory of Solly and Blanche.

About The Author

Angela Miller-Rothbart was born and raised in Paarl, South Africa. She is an entrepreneur and businesswoman. She is also an advanced Toastmaster. She is a mother of two daughters and has a grandson. Currently, she lives in Sea Point with her husband Henry.

This is her debut novel.